Tom Derringer and the Steam-Powered Saurians

OTHER NOVELS BY LAWRENCE WATT-EVANS

Tom Derringer

and the

Steam-Powered Saurians

Lawrence Watt-Evans

Misenchanted Press

Bainbridge Island

This is a work of fiction. None of the characters and events portrayed in this novel are intended to represent actual person living or dead.

Tom Derringer and the Steam-Powered Saurians

Published by Misenchanted Press
www.misenchantedpress.com

Cover design by Lawrence Watt-Evans & Connie Hirsch
Frontispieces by Kyrith Evans

Dedicated to

Isambard Kingdom Brunel

"By mid-morning, when we took our first real break, we were out of the city and well up the canyon road into the mountains."

"...we were traversing a narrow mountain pass where there was no smooth trail of a size to accommodate our vehicle."

TOM DERRINGER

Chapter One

I Meet Mr. Murray

Betsy Vanderhart and I arrived in San Francisco on the 4th of March, 1884, and took lodging in the Palace Hotel, as we had on our previous visit.

We were on our way to our homes back East after a series of adventures in and around and under Los Angeles, including finding ourselves caught up in what I was sure would become known as the Great Los Angeles Flood. We were in California because I am an adventurer by trade, like my father before me, and Miss Vanderhart was employed as my assistant, though our relationship was perhaps more than that simple statement might imply. I had been seeking a man named Gabriel Trask, and I had found him, though in the end nothing had come of it.

We took a steamer up the coast rather than heading directly east by rail for two reasons. The first of these was that the massive flooding had closed several of the rail lines in and out of Los Angeles, and we were unsure as to when they might be reliably back in service.

The second reason was that I had promised a dead man I would make contact with his employers and let them know what had become of him. Three of the five addresses he had provided me were in San Francisco, so I deemed it essential to visit that city before heading back East.

Even the sea route had presented challenges, though. I had been forced to pawn several items to raise the fare, since the lack of a functioning telegraph anywhere in Los Angeles had made it impossible to wire for funds. As it happens, before departing on our subterranean adventures I had left valuables sufficient to cover the cost at my hotel in Los Angeles, so we were able to take ship without undue delay. I was not especially concerned about how we would manage beyond that; I knew that once we had reached San Francisco my credit was good at the Palace.

I am fortunate that when my father died he left an estate sufficient to support his wife and children in comfort, if not luxury. Most adventurers do not manage this. Adventuring can be an expensive enterprise. Yes, the rewards can be rich, but for every expedition that returns laden with treasure several spend a fortune on equipment and travel and come back empty-handed. Often the proceeds of even a successful adventure are frittered away financing futile attempts to repeat the experience.

My parents had resisted that temptation. Their money was invested wisely with a family friend, a New York banker by the name of Tobias Arbuthnot, who had seen to it that our funds were carefully shepherded through whatever economic hazards might arise. Thus I had never suffered the indignities of poverty and had been able to train to follow in my father's footsteps without any great regard to the cost. What's more, before I even reached manhood I had been able to indulge myself in adventures that had little prospect of earning any return. My first had involved the purchase of an airship, the Vanderhart Aeronavigator, to investigate mysterious sightings in the skies of the Arizona Territory out of simple curiosity and with no thought of financial gain; the redoubtable Miss Vanderhart, daughter of the Aeronavigator's creator, had accompanied me as my engineer.

Our journey to Los Angeles had been the second occasion when Betsy accompanied me. I had not particularly needed an engineer this time, as the Aeronavigator had been lost in the jungles of the Yucatan, and we had relied on more mundane methods of transport, but Betsy's mother had reacted very poorly to some of her daughter's actions in Mexico. We had thought it best that the two have some time apart. Thus, Betsy had joined me on my trip to California.

Alas, we had been away from home for far longer than we had intended, having spent some months as prisoners of a tribe that was often referred to as "lizard people," but who were more properly known as the Skyless. Having escaped them at last, we had made our way to San Francisco.

We had come with little more than the clothes upon our backs, and it was only because the staff at the Palace knew me that we were permitted to take rooms in so fine an establishment despite our shabby appearance and dearth of baggage.

Even though we were suffering a serious lack of funds, not half an hour after we had checked in and assured ourselves that the little luggage we did possess was safely in our rooms, we headed out to the nearest Western Union office. It was not the need for money that compelled such haste, but the desire to let our families know we were still alive. They had not heard a word from us through all the months of our captivity, nor, thanks to the flood's depredations, since our escape.

Our finances were so limited that we had to keep our messages quite brief, saying only that we were alive and well, staying at the Palace, and in need of money.

That done, we retreated to our hotel, and in one of the parlors there I mentioned to my companion, "I am still awaiting a straight answer."

She had no need for further specifics; she knew what question I had asked when we had first regained our freedom. I had asked for her hand in marriage.

As I said, our relationship had become something more than the title "assistant" implied.

"Tom," she said, "I am not going to give you the answer you want. We have spent several months in each other's company, yes, but always under extraordinary circumstances. We have never had a chance to see one another in normal surroundings, amid family and friends. Nor have you had an opportunity to keep company with any other young ladies, or I, for that matter, other men. We are both young – indeed, you are younger than I by a year or so, if I am not mistaken – so I do not think there is any urgency in this. Let us both go about our business, and see what happens as we live our ordinary lives."

We were indeed young; I was still three months short of my eighteenth birthday. I thought, however, that I had found the role I would always play. "Betsy, my life may never be ordinary," I protested. "I am an adventurer, like my father before me!"

"But that is not an occupation I am eager to share!"

"You have certainly done splendidly at it so far."

She frowned, despite the sincere compliment. "Nonetheless, I do not care to continue. I like you, Tom, I won't deny it, even though I sometimes think you are the greatest fool I have ever met, but I have not enjoyed these past several months at all. If continuing to travel with you means a life filled with such experiences, then I prefer to forego the pleasure of your company. You hare off on the slightest whim, without any idea where you are going or what you hope to accomplish! That is no fit way to live."

"I made this most recent expedition to oblige *you*, so that you might escape your mother's wrath!" While I understood that Mrs. Vanderhart had some reason to be upset with the risks Betsy had taken in my company, upon learning that her daughter had shot Hezekiah McKee she had lost herself in a religious fervor that gone well beyond the limits of rationality, and I had entirely sympathized with Betsy's desire to be somewhere else.

"Indeed, I acknowledge as much, and I fault myself for not stopping it sooner."

I slumped back in my chair. I did not think further argument would do any good; in fact, I thought it likely to fix Betsy more firmly in the position she had taken.

I was not going to abandon my budding career as an adventurer, though; I had been training and preparing for it since the age of eight, when I had first discovered that my father, Jack Derringer, had been a member of the famed band led by Darien Lord, and that my mother had been the brave Arabella Whitaker who had sometimes accompanied them on their adventures.

But I could not deny the truth of all that Betsy had said.

This would require careful consideration.

For the moment I changed the subject, and after perhaps a quarter hour of desultory further conversation, we made our way to our separate rooms.

In the morning, after we had broken our fast in one of the hotel's excellent dining rooms, I announced my intention of calling upon one Benjamin Murray. His name was first on the list that the late John Beckwith had given me, and his address, on Franklin Street, was not impossibly far from the Palace. Our financial circumstances being what they were, I could afford neither hack nor cable car – yes, even a nickel fare was beyond me! I therefore had no choice but to walk; after consulting a map provided by the hotel, I estimated it to be a distance of perhaps two miles, which would scarcely be a serious hardship, but I offered Betsy the opportunity of staying at the hotel should she care to avoid the exertion.

She refused. "I am not about to miss an opportunity to make Mr. Murray's acquaintance," she said. I refrained from responding that it was this sort of enthusiasm that made me question her insistence that she wanted no further adventures.

Therefore, after outfitting ourselves as best we could in our diminished condition, we set out along Post Street.

The day was chilly and overcast, and after so long in the warmer climes of Los Angeles we were unaccustomed to such weather; I particularly regretted that I had left my hat in the tunnels of the so-called lizard people, and had not yet been able to replace it. To warm ourselves we walked quickly and did not speak at first. We passed Union Square and had gone another few blocks when Betsy asked, "What are you going to tell him?"

"That John Beckwith is dead," I said. "That was what I promised."

"And what are you going to say about where and how he died?"

"I'll..." I stopped in the middle of the street.

"You hadn't thought about it yet?"

"Not...not precisely," I admitted. "I would prefer to tell the truth."

"That Mr. Beckwith was killed by a poisoned dart shot by one of the lizard people in a secret tunnel beneath Los Angeles?"

"I...might not go into detail," I said.

"I think you should be prepared to face some questions, Tom. And I would not advise you to rely on your wits."

Annoyed by the implied slight, I said, "I have given it *some* thought."

"Well, good."

"But I want to see the situation before settling on my exact strategy. An adventurer must be able to improvise and to adjust his strategy on the fly in response to exigent circumstances."

"So you *do* plan to rely on your wits."

"To some extent, yes."

She shook her head. "It's your decision," she said.

I strode on along Post Street angrily leaving Betsy to catch up – I am perhaps an inch short of six feet in height, while she is scarcely an inch over five, so my natural stride is longer than hers, my pace quicker – but I relented and waited for her before crossing Taylor Street.

"Do you still think we are so suited to one another that you want to spend our lives together?" she asked as we crossed the street side by side.

I frowned and did not immediately reply. When at last we turned right onto Franklin Street, I answered, "I would not want a wife who meekly agreed with every word I said. I want a wife who will be my helpmeet, who will guide and advise me and keep me from making a fool of myself as often as I otherwise might. You seem ideally suited to that role, however uncomfortable I may find your guidance at times. I admit that I have sometimes been thoughtless and headstrong – and naive, let us not forget naive – and you have tempered those traits for me. I may not enjoy that tempering, but I know it's made me a better man and has almost certainly saved my life more than once. I am trying to be worthy of you, Betsy, but I am not there yet."

It was her turn to be silent for a few blocks, but as we approached the steps leading from the sidewalk up to the entry to our destination she said soberly, "That was a generous speech, Tom."

I had no reply to make beyond a wordless noise of acceptance and a shrug.

We made our way up to the little porch together, and I rang the bell, one of those modern mechanical ones worked by turning a handle in the middle of the door. While we awaited a response, Betsy and I found ourselves looking into one another's eyes.

But then the door opened, and a man in a morning coat said, "May I help you?"

"Ah," I said. I recognized the man as a butler, but was unsure of the proper way to greet such an individual; I had somehow survived to the ripe old age of seventeen without ever having had occasion to address a butler, and if it was ever discussed in my training I had forgotten it. I decided against extending a hand, and merely said, "Is Mr. Benjamin Murray in?"

"May I ask who is calling?"

"John Thomas Derringer, on behalf of Mr. John Beckwith." I started to reach for my vest pocket, then said, "I'm afraid I have run out of cards for the moment." In fact, my last few had been ruined by the floodwaters in Los Angeles – my card case had leaked. As I lowered my hand I remembered that I was not alone and I hastily added, "My delightful companion is Miss Elspeth Vanderhart."

"Very good, sir." He closed the door, leaving us to wait on the porch.

We waited silently, looking out at the neighborhood. Then the butler reappeared and ushered us inside, saying, "Mr. Murray is in the library."

The library, it seemed, was directly across the entry hall. The butler showed us to the door and announced us, then asked, "Shall I inform Mrs. Murray, sir?"

"That won't be necessary, Babson," a voice replied. "I am fairly certain this is not a social call."

"Tea, perhaps?"

"I think not."

"Very good, sir." The butler turned and vanished through a door to our left, allowing us to enter the library and meet our host.

We found a portly, bespectacled elderly gentleman on his feet, waiting for us; he came forward and took my hand. "Tom Derringer, the adventurer?" he said. "Jack Derringer's son?" I thought I detected the faintest lingering trace of an English accent.

"Yes, sir," I said. I stepped aside to introduce my companion. "And Elspeth Vanderhart, daughter of the famed Professor Vanderhart of Rutgers University."

Betsy curtseyed, and Mr. Murray said, "A pleasure to meet you, Miss Vanderhart. Please, won't you sit down?"

We took two red velvet chairs in front of a splendid bookcase, while Mr. Murray settled into a thronelike seat by the hearth, where a pleasant little fire danced. A photograph of our host accompanied by a woman and four children, presumably his family, stood on the mantel.

"Now," he said, "what can I do for you? You mentioned a Mr. Beckwith? I don't believe I know anyone by that name."

"Oh," I said. "Perhaps you knew him only by his other professional name, Justus Smith."

"Ah," Mr. Murray replied, steepling his fingers. "I do recognize *that* name, yes. Did you say you came on his behalf?"

"At his request, at any rate. He asked me to inform his employers of his fate and gave me a list of five names. Yours was the first of those."

Mr. Murray adjusted his glasses. "His fate," he said. "And what fate is this?"

"I regret to say, Mr. Murray, that Mr. Beckwith, whom you knew by the name Smith, died in late January of this year."

Mr. Murray reached a hand under his coat; from the corner of my eye I saw Betsy tense, one of her own hands moving toward her bosom. "And was this your doing, Mr. Derringer?" Murray asked.

"No, sir, it was not. Mr. Beckwith and I had made our peace with one another, and I had invited him to join our party, so that he could see for himself that we were not hunting Emperor Norton's imaginary treasure."

The late Joshua Norton had declared himself Emperor of the United States and Protector of Mexico in 1859, and the people of San Francisco had seen fit to humor this until his death in 1880. Although poor Mr. Norton had lived off the charity of his friends, there were those who had thought he had a secret hoard hidden away somewhere, and at least one such individual had thought that my own sojourn in California was in pursuit of this mythical treasure trove and had hired John Beckwith to follow me in hopes of sharing in whatever I might discover.

As I have mentioned, I had actually been seeking a man named Gabriel Trask, and had found him in the tunnels beneath Los Angeles. There was no lost imperial treasury.

Mr. Murray withdrew his hand, without bringing forth a pistol; Betsy fiddled with her collar. "Then what *did* befall the gentleman in question?"

"My actual mission, Mr. Murray, was to locate a man I believed to be living with one of the local native tribes in southern California. We were successful in this, but alas, the tribe in question doubted our good intentions and held us prisoner. Mr. Beckwith was killed trying to escape – struck in the throat by a poisoned dart. Miss Vanderhart and I were more careful and contrived our own escape perhaps three weeks later, aided by the fierce storms and flooding that I am sure you have heard about."

Mr. Murray considered this silently for a moment, then looked at Betsy. "And you, Miss Vanderhart – do you confirm Mr. Derringer's story? If he is holding you against your will, this would be a perfect opportunity to free yourself; I can protect you."

Betsy laughed. "I assure you, Mr. Murray, I wouldn't need your help to escape from Tom! I am here of my own free will, and yes, Tom has told you the truth. The tribe in question calls itself the *Kyinhuk*, I believe. Mr. Beckwith had managed to shoot his guard in the leg but was apprehended and killed before he could flee."

Kyinhuk was the word for "Skyless" in the lizard people's own tongue, Kanta'an; I confess I could probably not have recalled it, and I feared that in any case I could not have pronounced it as well as she did. At first I thought that naming them was foolish, given that we wanted to keep their location and nature secret, but then I realized it was not foolish at all; Mr. Murray would never associate the word with any legends he might have heard about the lizard people and their tunnels, and indeed, this other name might well distract him from any unwelcome notions about our captors.

"I see," Mr. Murray said. "And what became of Mr. Trask? At least, I assume it was he you were seeking."

"It was," I admitted. "He had been an honored guest among the *Kyinhuk*, but I'm afraid they blamed him, in part, for Mr. Beckwith's actions. He escaped with us, and we parted ways in Los Angeles." I discovered that my fears had been correct; my pronunciation was not as accurate as Betsy's, though there was no way Mr. Murray could know which of us was more nearly correct.

"So there was no lost treasure that Trask was hiding for Emperor Norton?" he asked, his head tilted to one side.

"Not a cent," I assured him. "I was seeking Mr. Trask because I had heard him accused of certain crimes, and I wanted to know whether the accusation was true, and whether he should be brought to justice. He convinced me that the accusation was unfounded – indeed, that it could not possibly be true, given his circumstances."

"Ah. I could wish I had known that beforehand; Mr. Smith might still be alive."

"I told anyone who asked that I was not after treasure," I pointed out, trying to keep any sense of grievance out of my tone of voice. "I was not believed."

"True enough. Well, this is all very unfortunate." He shook his head. "*Very* unfortunate. Especially because we had another job for Mr. Smith, had he survived."

"Excuse me," Betsy interjected. "Who is *we?*"

"Oh, I assumed that Mr. Smith had told you that when he gave Mr. Derringer that list of names," he said, looking first at her, and then at me. "We are a...a sort of committee. Not a vigilance committee like those of thirty years ago, which I suppose you are familiar with, but in something of the same spirit, albeit on a far smaller scale. We do not concern ourselves with common crimes, and political corruption is of only secondary interest to us; we merely try to ensure that adventurers active in this part of the United States restrict themselves to relatively benign undertakings. We are not adventurers ourselves, you understand – you could hardly expect a man of my age to go gallivanting about the countryside battling miscreants or hunting for treasure! But we make an effort to ensure that no one tries to stir up trouble, or destroys any landmarks, or otherwise disrupts the good order of the republic."

"Something like the Order of Theseus?" I asked, referring to the famous brotherhood of adventurers.

"Not...well, there may be some similarities, but no, not really. We simply try to keep track of all the adventurers in the area, and we try to be aware of their intentions, in case it seems prudent to intervene."

"And if the occasion arises that you can enrich yourself in the process by taking a share of any discovered treasures, that's a welcome extra?" Betsy asked.

Mr. Murray let out a snort of laughter. "I can see you're a clever girl!" he said. "Yes, I admit that our committee is not entirely selfless. We've profited from our investigations and intend to continue to do so. We have encouraged treasure-hunting adventurers, and even funded them on occasion, as well as trying to stop the troublemakers."

"And which is this job you were going to offer Mr. Beckwith?" I asked.

"I do wish you'd call him Smith," Mr. Murray said. "I never knew him as Beckwith and can't quite get used to it."

"Mr. Smith, then. Was this job one of peacekeeping, or one of treasure seeking?"

"Some of both, I'd say," Mr. Murray said. "Do you remember Teddy Hancock?"

Betsy and I exchanged glances. "We've met him," I said. We had, in fact, encountered my fellow adventurer, Edward "Steady Teddy" Hancock, on the train on our journey west. Prior to that I had known him only by reputation.

"Of course you have; how do you think we got on your trail in the first place? Our committee was backing his little expedition in the Utah Territory, so he reported your presence to our agents in Ogden."

Several details from last year's travels fell into place and made more sense than they had heretofore. "I see," I said.

Mr. Murray eyed me thoughtfully. "Perhaps *you* might consider taking the job, if my fellow committee members approve."

"You still haven't said what it is."

"Why, finding Teddy Hancock, of course," Mr. Murray said. "He's gone missing."

Chapter Two

An Offer of Employment

"Missing?" I said. "Where?"

"If we knew that, then he wouldn't be missing, would he?" Mr. Murray asked. "The last we knew he was headed east out of Ogden, into the Wasatch Mountains. We expected him back by Christmas, but we haven't heard a word."

"It seems as if you've been losing more people than usual lately," Betsy remarked.

"Indeed it does," Mr. Murray agreed. "Nor were these two the only ones to drop out of sight of late, merely the only two in our employ. We don't like it. Whether this is mere coincidence or a part of something greater we do not know, and that concerns us. We decided, at our last gathering just a few days ago, that should either Smith or Hancock turn up, we would send him after the other. Well, you tell us Smith is dead – would you consider taking his place in seeking Mr. Hancock?"

"I believe Smith had a partner, by the name of Andrew Bowlby," I said. "Why have you not hired him for this?"

"They were not exactly *partners*, just two men we hired for the same job. Mr. Bowlby is not interested in working outside the San Francisco area; that was part of why he did not accompany Mr. Smith to Los Angeles. He also does not enjoy a reputation like your own; he is, in fact, if I must be honest, somewhat slow witted and far too fond of liquor. No, he is not suitable, so I will repeat my question – would *you* consider seeking Mr. Hancock for us?"

"I should need to know more about the situation before deciding," I said.

"Of course, of course! And I would need to consult with my colleagues before employing you. Where are you staying?"

"At the Palace Hotel."

"Of course you are. I should have known. And will you be there long?"

"A few days, at the least."

"But we were planning to return to the East soon," Betsy added.

"Well, Ogden is on your way, then."

"But the mountains east of it are not," she replied.

"True, but a little side trip would be profitable, and of service to a fellow adventurer."

"How profitable?" Betsy and I asked, almost in unison. While my situation was such that I did not really need to earn my living, I was becoming uncomfortably aware of the strain I had placed on my family's finances, especially given the recent financial setbacks and large price increases that the country as a whole was suffering at the time. My father's investments had not been as successful of late as they had been when I was a child, and I had been spending significant sums on my adventures – spending rather recklessly, in fact.

"That remains to be seen. If you could see fit to remain at the Palace for, oh, a week, I should have a decision by then, and would make you a more specific offer, as well as informing you of the details of Mr. Hancock's quest, his last known whereabouts, and whatever else may seem relevant."

"Fair enough," I said. "A week it is." I hesitated. "Did Mr. Smith have any family who should be informed of his demise? He gave me only the list of five names - three here in San Francisco, one in Sacramento, and one in Salt Lake City."

"I am not aware of any living relatives, but I will look into it. The locations you give for those five would accord with the directors of our committee. I assume that besides myself, your list is comprised of Messrs. Holzmann, Clement, Dobbs, and Cartwright?"

"That is correct, sir."

He nodded. "That is the entire permanent membership of our little company. Other associates may come and go as circumstances dictate. You need not worry that the list is incomplete in any significant way, and I do not know of any family or friends who should be informed."

"Then we have taken enough of your time." I rose. "Thank you for seeing us."

"Thank *you* for bringing me the unhappy news," he replied. "And you need not call on the others on that list; I will see that they are informed."

I nodded, then held out a hand; Betsy took it and got to her feet.

"You'll be hearing from us," Mr. Murray called after us as we left the room.

The butler met us at the library door and escorted us out.

When we were on the sidewalk and walking south along Franklin, Betsy said, "Will you take the job?"

"I haven't decided," I said. "The offered payment remains undefined, and there are many other details to be discussed."

After a few steps in silence, she said, "Then we have no commitments for the next week?"

"Oh, I still plan to call on the next two men on the list," I replied.

"What? Why?"

"Because I prefer not to take Mr. Murray at his word until I know his word is good. He admitted that he and his compatriots operate in secret and manipulate adventurers to their own benefit; why should I assume that anything he tells us is true? He may well be hoping to exclude his fellow committee members from whatever he has planned, or to otherwise shortchange them. Indeed, he may not have believed a word we said and may already be setting spies and assassins on our trail. Or he may have lied to us from the start; there may not *be* any committee, and the connection between him and Beckwith's other employers may be something else entirely. Why, we cannot even be certain that was the real Benjamin Murray! For all we know, those two men murdered Murray and his butler and took their places."

"Tom, that's nonsense.

"Is it?"

"Of course it is. Didn't you see the picture above the fireplace?"

"Perhaps these impostors brought it with them to add a little verisimilitude to their story."

"That is *completely* preposterous."

"Is it?" I repeated. But then I shrugged. "I suppose it probably is. But in the past I have been too trusting, as you have not hesitated to tell me, and if I am perhaps now moving too far toward the opposite extreme, is that not the safer approach?"

She stared at me without replying, then turned her gaze forward.

We were crossing California Street a moment later when I added, "Besides, would you not enjoy meeting two more of these supposed puppet masters?"

I could see her struggling not to smile. Instead of answering, she said, "I thought you did a good job of telling Mr. Murray how Mr. Smith died, without giving away any secrets in the process."

"Thank you. I thought *you* did a good job of adding corroborative detail."

And with that the tension between us was lessened; for the remainder of the walk back to the Palace we chatted casually about the weather, our surroundings, and other lighter matters. Betsy remarked on the rumble and clang of the passing cable cars and mentioned that she would like an opportunity to see more of the mechanisms that pulled them through the streets – her engineering curiosity had been aroused. I regretted that we could not as yet spare the cost of the fare and promised myself that before we left town I would see to it that she had a chance to ride one, and in a seat that gave her a view of the gripman's labors.

The air had warmed somewhat, and the overcast was thinning, which also made our journey more pleasant, and we arrived back at the Palace perhaps a little footsore, but all in all in a very good mood.

We took our lunch in the hotel's American Dining Room, the establishment's most celebrated restaurant, and as we emerged after our meal a bellboy caught us to let us know that I had received a telegram and could pick it up at the front desk.

It was, of course, from my mother, and she had clearly not worried about the cost, as it was three pages long, letting me know that she and my sister Mary Ann were well, and that she would inform our friends, and Betsy's family, that we were still alive. She admitted that there had been great concern about our long silence.

She assured me that she would wire funds to me as soon as it could be arranged with our banker, Toby Arbuthnot.

And finally, she asked that I let her know my plans and whether I would be returning home soon. She said I had been greatly missed at Christmas, and that she hoped, if it was practical, that I might be home for Easter.

I was unutterably pleased to receive this missive, with all its familiar names and maternal reassurances; it let me know that I had indeed returned to the normal modern world after our months underground, and that it had not been severely altered in my absence.

"Is there a reply, Mr. Derringer?" the clerk asked.

"Not at present," I replied. "Thank you." I did not care to admit that I could not even afford a tip for the bellboy. I could have charged a telegram to my hotel account, I suppose, but I preferred not to add any unnecessary costs. I would stop by the Western Union office later, to see whether Mr. Arbuthnot had sent the requested funds.

I was turning away from the desk when Betsy asked forlornly, "Was there no telegram for me?"

Startled, the clerk turned and checked his boxes. Then he turned back and said, "I'm afraid not, Miss Vanderhart."

"Thank you," she said, and we headed out across the lobby.

I could see that she was hurt that her parents had not answered her own telegram. We had made a point of wiring both households, despite our dwindling resources.

We had come west largely to give Betsy's mother time to regain her composure. When she had learned that her daughter had killed a man in self-defense she had gone into a positive tizzy, developing a sort of religious mania and demanding her daughter beg God's forgiveness and behave as a penitent. Betsy had declined to cooperate, and when her father went off to the South Seas on some sort of scientific expedition, removing his moderating influence, Betsy had been unable to stand her mother's behavior any longer and had fled to my side. We had undertaken the journey to California, with Betsy in the role of my assistant, so that she might, without setting tongues wagging, avoid going home. I had put my faith in the old adage that absence makes the heart grow fonder and had trusted that Mrs. Vanderhart would come to her senses.

The lack of a telegram seemed a sign that no such repentance had taken place and that Betsy was still an outcast.

"Are you going to wire your mother again?" Betsy asked.

"Not immediately," I said. "I would prefer to know more about my prospects of employment first."

"Oh." That seemed to end her interest in further conversation.

We returned to our rooms to rest and refresh ourselves, with a rendezvous set for 2:00 to be followed by a walk to the second address on the list, that of a Mr. Abner Holzmann who lived in the district of the city known as Russian Hill. Our rendezvous accomplished exactly on schedule, we set out, once again required by our temporary poverty to rely upon shank's mare.

The weather was even more greatly improved, the overcast broken into scattered clouds. The distance was scarcely more than that to Mr. Murray's establishment, but the route we chose proved to take us through a more crowded part of the city, as well as up some rather intimidating slopes, so that the journey required slightly more than an hour. We arrived and rang the bell, and were admitted by a housekeeper, rather than a butler, who showed us into a tidy, sunlit parlor.

Mr. Holzmann turned out to be a diminutive fellow, not much taller than Betsy, with black hair the color of cheap shoe polish, and a flamboyant mustache. He was perched on the edge of a brocade settee, with a small pile of papers beside him. He invited us to make ourselves at home, and we settled upon two convenient chairs.

Once we had seated ourselves, he said, "So you're Tom Derringer."

"Yes, sir." I gestured at my companion. "And this is Miss Elspeth Vanderhart."

"Ben Murray said you were in town." He tapped the papers. "I just had a note from him, not half an hour ago, asking me to meet him tomorrow to discuss your arrival."

"I see," I said. "And did Mr. Murray explain why I came?"

"He says you had some tale about Justus Smith getting himself killed by wild Indians somewhere down near the Mexican border."

"I believe we were closer to Los Angeles than to Mexico," I

said mildly.

"But that's the tale, is it?　Shot through the neck with a poisoned arrow?"

"More of a dart than an arrow," I said. "He had shot his guard in the leg, and the report of his pistol attracted the other men of the tribe."

Mr. Holzmann nodded. "So we had the gist of it. And since you had already conveyed this to Ben Murray, as you supposedly promised our late employee, why are you *here?*"

"I promised Mr. Smith that I would see to it that all five of his employers were informed of his tragic demise. I have nothing against Mr. Murray, sir, but I don't know him, I never made his acquaintance before today, and I did not care to rely on his assurance that he would accurately relay the details. Furthermore, I wished to give you the opportunity to ask any questions you might have about the unhappy events of the last few months."

"And you probably don't mind having a chance to look *me* over, either.　Ben says he wants to hire you to find Teddy Hancock for us, and I daresay you want to know who you'd be working for. Am I right?"

"I cannot deny it," I said.

"That's good sense. Well, here I am – what do you make of me?"

"You seem to be a direct sort of fellow," I said. I did not add, though I could have, that he also seemed to think very highly of himself, and not to be very concerned with details; I doubted that Mr. Murray had garbled my account of Mr. Beckwith's death as badly as what Mr. Holzmann had just told us.

"Direct! Yes! That's the word for it, isn't it? By George, direct!" He slapped his hand on the back of the settee. "And that being said, Mr. Derringer, let me ask you a direct question – is this story you've brought us the whole truth? We sent Smith after treasure – did he find any?"

"No, Mr. Holzmann, he did not. I assure you that the tribe

we found, the *Kyinhuk*, the tribe hosting Gabriel Trask, was miserably poor. They had no money of any kind, not even for use among themselves; in all the time we spent among them we never saw a single golden ornament or silver trinket, or a coin of any description." I carefully did not mention their sacred archives, which were engraved on sheets of solid gold; they had no coins or other golden objects because the precious metal was reserved for the holy records. Nor did I give any explanation of the marvels of their underground civilization, with its phosphorescent fungus and rock-shaping chemicals. "Mr. Trask was staying with them as much out of pity as anything else, I'd say," I continued. "Certainly not in hope of becoming wealthy. I'd gone looking for Trask because I'd heard it said he was the late Emperor Norton's spymaster, and I thought he might have some secrets worth knowing, but after talking to him I don't believe he was. I think it was a misunderstanding."

"Well, that's a shame."

"Indeed. I'll be direct with *you*, Mr. Holzmann – I wish there *had* been some treasure; I came away with not two dollars in my pocket and have had to wire my family for more funds. When I told Mr. Murray that I would be at the Palace for a few more days, that's because I won't be able to pay my bill until that money arrives."

"You don't say! Well, maybe our offer of employment will suit you, then."

"It very well might, Mr. Holzmann, and I look forward to hearing the details and negotiating the terms." I rose. "But I won't keep you. Thank you for your consideration."

Mr. Holzmann himself showed us out, the housekeeper apparently being occupied elsewhere. When we were on the sidewalk outside and beginning our walk back to our hotel, I remarked, "You never said a word."

"And he never said a word to me, nor looked at me, even when you introduced me," Betsy replied. "I suppose he thought I was your kept woman and beneath his notice."

"What sort of man would bring his mistress along on an errand like this?" I exclaimed.

"A foolish one - which he probably believes you to be."

"Do you think so? It's best to be underestimated."

"Who ever said anything about underestimating you?" Her little bow of a mouth was drawn up in a lopsided smile, and I grinned back.

But then her smile vanished. "Do you think it wise to tell him about your financial situation?"

"Ah, but I didn't, not really. I told him we are temporarily impoverished, which he could probably find out for himself with a few discreet questions, and that we are relying on funds from back East, but I gave him no information about just how easily my dear mother can replenish our exchequer. He probably believes it will be a strain on our family's resources, and that I may be desperate for this job they're dangling before us, and that might be useful in negotiating."

"I would think it would be more useful if they thought you *didn't* need the job."

"Oh, I don't think so. In that case, if I appeared uninterested they might just find someone else. You'll see, I hope."

"I hope so, too." She looked up the street ahead, and at the sky above, which was clouding over again. "Will we be visiting the third man today? The afternoon is half over."

"I think not." I pulled Beckwith's note from my pocket. "This third address is on the far side of the city, almost overlooking the Pacific Ocean, which is farther than I care to walk today - especially since we cannot hope to dine on credit anywhere but the Palace, and we still have no money. I am hoping that Mr. Arbuthnot will remedy that some time tomorrow, and we can hire a hack to take us to Mr. Clement's establishment, or perhaps find a cable car route that will get us there."

"That suits me," she said.

"Shall we stop by the telegraph office on our way back to the Palace and see if there is any word from your family?"

"I doubt there will be, but I don't suppose it will do any harm to stop in."

"Then we shall." I looked down at her, huddling in her little jacket against the chill and damp, and wished we could stop into a shop and buy her a wrap or cloak, but we did not yet have any way to pay for one. Instead I picked up the pace a trifle, so that the activity might warm our blood, and we marched briskly through the streets.

Chapter Three

Our Circumstances Improve

To my surprise, there *was* something waiting for us at the Western Union office, but it was not a wire from the Vanderharts; instead it was the sum of $400, accompanied by a brief message from our family banker, Toby Arbuthnot: REQUESTED FUNDS ATTACHED STOP ARABELLA SAYS URGENT SO RUSHED SERVICE STOP EAGER TO HEAR DETAILS WHEN YOU RETURN NEW YORK STOP.

I felt an unaccustomed warmth at the reminder that I had friends and family who cared about me. I took the time to compose a return message, thanking him, and then also wrote a longer telegram to my mother, reassuring her once again that we were fine and explaining that although the business that had brought me to California was done I might be accepting a job that could delay me for some time, and therefore could not say with certainty when I would be home.

I also asked, after making sure Betsy was distracted and not watching what I wrote, whether Mother had heard anything from the Vanderharts.

It was a relief to be able to send these messages without having to count every word to be sure I had the necessary cash.

That done, we proceeded to our hotel.

Immediately after breakfast the following day I began making arrangements to hire an agent who would deal with my creditors in Los Angeles, in some cases ransoming possessions I had left as security. While I did that Betsy took a portion of our replenished funds and visited several shops, so that she might add to her sadly diminished wardrobe. Taking inspiration from her example, once I had completed my negotiations I made my way down Market Street to buy myself a new hat.

Though the item itself was an unremarkable derby I felt much more myself, once again a civilized gentleman, in my new headgear – and more protected, as the skies were gray and rain seemed likely. I cannot say that San Francisco's March weather had endeared itself to me.

Once reunited, after I had admired those of her purchases that she allowed me to see, we took luncheon, and then proceeded to the hotel entry to engage a hack. I had determined, after consulting maps and the concierge, that even the Geary Street, Park, and Ocean cable cars did not come within a dozen blocks of our destination. I gave the driver the address, and we settled back on the leather seats for the ride across town.

"It's good to be back to ourselves," I said, adjusting my new hat.

"Back to ourselves?" Betsy said. "Is that how it seems to you?"

I looked at her, startled. "Well, yes," I said.

She slumped back and crossed her arms over her bosom, pulling a new shawl around her. "I suppose it is," she said. "Here I am, riding hither and yon on errands of which I don't approve – yes, that's what I've done far too often."

"Betsy, if I have done or said something to offend you, I sincerely beg your pardon. I can tell the driver to return to the hotel, if you like."

She shook her head and remained silent for several seconds

before saying, "It's not you, Tom. It's my parents. Ever since I turned twelve, my father sent me everywhere from Richmond to Montreal on his errands – and then finally to Flagstaff, to help you with the Aeronavigator. It seems I've spent half my life on trains or in cabs or in the parlors of strangers. I have never been allowed any time for myself. Do you know I've never been to a dance? I'm eighteen, and have never been to a dance!"

"Oh," I said. "Ah – neither have I."

She looked at me from beneath lowered brows. "Really?"

"Really," I said. "I did have dancing lessons, so that I might hold my own should the occasion arise, but I have never danced with anyone but my mother, my sister, and my dancing master."

She stared at me for a moment, frowning.

"I was set on becoming an adventurer, you see, like my father before me," I said. "I learned to shoot and fight and track, to speak six languages, to decipher hidden messages, and to read treasure maps. I studied history and legend, and geography both ordinary and mystical, and other such things, and that did not leave me much time for dances or parties."

She considered this for a few seconds, then said, "You *chose* that."

"Yes, I did. And you did not ask to be your father's messenger and mechanician; I understand that our circumstances were quite different. Still, we have both missed out on some common experiences."

"I suppose," she said, turning away, "but *your* mother still loves you."

I could only sit in helpless silence after that. I could think of nothing to say that might not make matters worse. I was tempted to throw my arms around her and offer her whatever comfort there might be in my embrace, but I had no right to do so. She had not accepted my proposal of marriage, nor otherwise indicated that such an intimacy would be welcome.

The silence grew longer and less comfortable and dragged on

for what seemed an eternity before our driver finally called to his
horse and brought the vehicle to a stop.

"Here you are, folks," he said. "This is the address you gave
me."

We disembarked, and I paid him; then we turned to the
house and marched up the steps.

The bell brought an aide or manservant of some sort; his
attire was far less formal than that of Mr. Murray's man, so I was
not certain whether he was a butler or some other functionary. At
any rate, he opened the door and started to say something, then
stopped.

"You aren't Mr. Holzmann," he said.

"That's very astute of you," I said. The long silent ride had
left me irritable. "I'm Tom Derringer, here to see Mr. Clement."

"He's just about to go out, but...wait here." He vanished back
into the house.

We waited on the stoop. A moment later he reappeared.
"This way," he said, and swung the door wide.

We followed him into a sitting room where a tall red-headed
man in a cashmere overcoat stood waiting. Gloves, a walking
stick, and a top hat sat upon a nearby table, indicating that he
really had been about to go out. He held out a hand.

"Mr. Derringer," he said. "I've heard so much about you."
He took my hand, then looked over my shoulder. "And this must
be Miss Vanderhart?"

"Yes," I said. "You are Adrian Clement?"

"I am. And to what do I owe the pleasure of this visit?"

"I promised the late John Beckwith, whom I believe you
knew as Justus Smith, that I would inform you of the
circumstances of his death. I have come to do so."

"But you must know that I've had a letter on the matter from
Ben Murray!"

"I promised Mr. Beckwith that I would see you myself. I
keep my promises."

"Well, that's very admirable, I'm sure. I have been told he was struck in the throat with a poisoned dart while attempting to escape from a local tribe somewhere outside Los Angeles; is that correct?"

"It is." I noted that *this* man had the details exactly right, unlike Mr. Holzmann.

"I do not feel the need of any further details, Mr. Derringer, though I appreciate your conscientiousness. Was there anything else?"

"I wanted to get a look at you, sir, since it's possible I may soon be working for you and your fellows."

"Indeed." He seemed somewhat taken aback by this.

Just then a bell jingled, and we heard footsteps.

"That will be Abbie Holzmann," our host said. "As a matter of fact, Mr. Derringer, we are on our way to a meeting with Mr. Murray at the Grand Hotel to discuss whether or not to hire you. We chose the site to be convenient, should we need to reach you – as I'm sure you know, the Grand is just across the street from the Palace."

The servant reappeared in the doorway and announced, "Mr. Holzmann is here."

"Tell him I'll be right there," Mr. Clement said. "Was there anything else, Mr. Derringer? I don't wish to keep him waiting."

"A quick question, if I may. Mr. Murray said that you and the other four men on the list Mr. Smith gave me constitute a self-appointed committee to regulate the activities of adventurers in northern California and in the Utah Territory. Is that correct?"

"More or less. I would not say 'regulate' so much as 'monitor,' though."

"Do you coordinate at all with the archivist Mr. John Pierce in New York?"

Again, he seemed taken aback. "No, Mr. Derringer, we do not. Perhaps we could discuss this further at another time? Mr. Holzmann is waiting."

"Of course. Pardon me." I stepped aside.

Betsy cleared her throat.

Mr. Clement looked at her, then glanced out the window at the street. Dark spots were appearing on the dirt as fat raindrops fell. "Ah," he said. "Perhaps, if Mr. Holzmann does not consider it too great an imposition, we might offer you a ride back to your hotel?"

"That would be most welcome, sir," I said.

Abner Holzmann was somewhat startled to see us come down the steps and approach his carriage, but after the initial surprise had passed, he burst out, "Ha! You've followed through, have you, Mr. Derringer? Visited all of us, just as you said you would. And I suppose you'll be seeing Dobbs and Cartwright?"

"I have not yet decided whether that will be necessary, sir, since I have no other business in Sacramento or Salt Lake City. I may make do with letters, rather than visiting them in person."

"A reasonable approach! But here we all are now; are we giving you a ride back to your hotel? We are? Well, welcome aboard!" He slid aside, making room on the benches. The three of us clambered into the vehicle. As soon as we were seated the coachman whipped up the horses, and we began rolling.

After a brief silence, I said, "Pardon me, gentlemen, but I would have thought it would make more sense to start at Mr. Clement's residence and pass by Mr. Holzmann's, rather than the reverse."

"I had business out this way," Mr. Holzmann replied. "And a better carriage, as well! Adrian's bounces like an Irishman dancing a jig."

"I see." I glanced at Mr. Clement to see whether he would offer a defense, but he seemed content to let Mr. Holzmann's explanation stand. In fact, Mr. Holzmann's carriage did seem exceptionally well sprung; we hardly felt the bumps in the streets, a pleasant change from our westbound trip.

Mr. Holzmann grinned. "Wouldn't want to bruise the little

lady, would we?"

I did not deign to answer this sally; Betsy pointedly turned her face away to gaze out the carriage window.

We made the rest of the journey mostly in silence, though every so often Mr. Clement or Mr. Holzmann would make some trivial remark about the weather, or about the neighborhoods we were passing through.

And then we were on Market Street, approaching Montgomery, and Mr. Holzmann leaned out the window to direct the driver to the grand entrance to the Palace. There the carriage came to a halt, and the driver leapt down to assist Betsy to the ground. I followed, and Mr. Holzmann closed the door behind me.

"Stay where the bellboys can find you, Derringer," he called. "You should be hearing from us before suppertime."

Then the driver scrambled back to his perch and shook the reins, and the coach rolled on – though it hardly seemed worth making a separate stop when the Grand was, indeed, directly across the street.

We watched the carriage go, and then Betsy and I made our way into the hotel, where we settled in one of the public parlors. I was debating whether or not to summon an attendant to bring me a newspaper, but I had hardly sat down when Betsy remarked, "I don't much care for Mr. Holzmann."

"I can't say I do, either," I responded.

"Then are you still considering working for these men?"

"I'm considering it, yes. It's not a certainty, by any means."

"No?"

"No, of course not. I know they want someone to find Teddy Hancock, but I don't know what they're paying, or where he went, or why, or what information they can provide about him. I'm not about to spend months or years wandering around the mountains with no idea of how I might locate Mr. Hancock, nor am I going to accept any job where the pay is insultingly low, and if they demand close oversight I might well consider that a good reason to say no. I don't mind taking Mr. Holzmann's money, but I don't want to spend much time with him."

"The others aren't so bad."

"No, they aren't. I rather liked what I saw of Mr. Clement, and if Mr. Murray hadn't reached for his pistol I might have said the same about him."

"Well, he had no way of knowing what to expect from you! He set Smith on your trail with orders to steal any treasure you might find; is it really so unlikely that you would take umbrage, kill Mr. Smith, and then come after whoever sent him?"

"I suppose not."

"Are you really sure he was reaching for a gun?"

"Aren't you? I saw you going for yours!"

"Well, I thought he *might* be," Betsy admitted. "Do you think he knew I had the derringer?"

"Probably not. If he *did* think you carried one, he most likely would have expected it to be in your handbag, not your blouse."

"I didn't *have* a handbag," she pointed out.

"Then he probably thought you were unarmed. *I* was, after all."

"Are you going to buy a new gun?"

I had lost both my Colt pistol and my Winchester rifle in the tunnels beneath Los Angeles and had not yet replaced them. "That depends," I said. "If we take this job hunting Teddy Hancock, I'm certainly not going after him without firearms and ammunition. If we go straight home, though, I don't see any great need for weapons."

"That's what we'll do if you don't take the job? Go straight home?"

"Well, yes," I said, startled. "What else would we do?"

"*I* don't know," she said, looking away. "You don't have some other adventure to undertake?"

"Not really, no."

"No other mysterious strangers to track down? No lost cities to visit, or would-be conquerors to stymie?"

"No. Certainly not without taking time to rest and resupply."

She fell silent, hands folded in her lap, eyes downcast.

"You don't want to go home," I said.

She did not answer.

"You know, they may not have received your telegram," I said. "Perhaps your father has not yet returned from Sumatra, and perhaps your mother was traveling. We didn't pay for warranted delivery, and it's only been a couple of days."

She raised her gaze – not to me, but to the piano on the far side of the room. "It's possible," she said. "It *is* possible, isn't it?"

"Of course it is."

She still did not look at me.

"Betsy," I said, "it really *is* possible. But even if they did get the wire, even if they are being the heartless beasts you seem to think, even if you are no longer welcome in New Brunswick, you will *always* be welcome in *my* home, and at my mother's hearth. We can find a way to minimize any scandal, I'm sure."

"If you think I'm going to marry you to keep tongues from wagging, Tom Derringer..."

I held up a hand. "Miss Vanderhart," I said, "I do not want you to marry me unless you are not merely willing, but *eager* to be my partner for the rest of our lives, until death do us part. I love you, and I want you to be happy, whether with me or without me. It saddens me to see you so miserable."

She stared at the piano for another few seconds, then said, "I believe that's the first time you have said that you love me."

"Was it? Please pardon the oversight. I do love you, Betsy."

"I don't know that you know what the word means."

"I don't know that I do, either," I admitted. "But I think I have it right."

She finally allowed herself a small smile. "I believe I'll go up to my room," she said. "You don't need me around while you bargain with the committee."

"I would appreciate your insight," I said. "As you have often told me, I sometimes lack common sense."

"I suspect those gentlemen would just as soon not have a lady present during negotiations."

I could not really argue with that. "As you please, then. Shall I see you at supper?"

"We shall see, Mr. Derringer," she said. She got to her feet and repeated, "We shall see."

I rose as well, as a gentleman should, and watched her go. Then I returned to the lobby to find a newspaper.

Chapter Four

The Nature of the Job

Iwas still reading the paper, but had worked my way down to
the minor notices of shipping arrivals, engagements, and the
like, when a boy found me.

"Mr. Derringer," he said, "there are three men here to see
you."

"Excellent!" I said, folding the newspaper. "Show me to
them."

A moment or two later the four of us were seated around a
table in the quietest of the hotel's three ground-floor parlors. Mr.
Clement glanced around and said, "Do you think this is
sufficiently private?"

"Oh, it'll do fine," Mr. Holzmann said. "Sit down and stop
worrying; we aren't going to be revealing any great secrets."

"There may be a confidential matter or two," Mr. Murray
murmured. "Does it suit *you*, Mr. Derringer?"

"I'm fine, gentlemen. Am I to take it, from your presence in
person rather than a simple message, that you have agreed to
employ me to locate Mr. Hancock?"

"That is correct," Mr. Murray said.

"We'll pay you four hundred dollars if you bring him back

alive," Mr. Holzmann said.

"And what if he is not alive?" I asked.

Holzmann looked uncomfortable.

"Four hundred dollars, alive or dead," Mr. Clement said, with an angry glance at Holzmann. "Another hundred bonus if he's alive and well."

"Bring him back," I said. "To where? To the best of my knowledge, Mr. Hancock has never set foot in San Francisco."

"True enough," Mr. Murray agreed. "Get him to Ogden, and that will suffice."

"We have a man there," Clement said. "You'll meet with him."

"That would be Peter Cartwright, perhaps?" I asked.

"He's on your list, is he?" Holzmann asked.

"Yes, though his address is given as Salt Lake City."

"Pete moves around," Holzmann said.

"That's fine, then – I am to bring Mr. Hancock to Ogden, for the sum of five hundred dollars."

"Four," Holzmann protested.

"Five, with the bonus. Let me make it clear, gentlemen, that if you hire me, you are hiring a skilled adventurer. You may think I'm too young to know much about the trade, but I have been studying and training under the tutelage of Arabella Whitaker, formerly of Darien Lord's company, since I was a boy of eight. I have studied my father's career in detail, including his secret personal records. I have flown an airship the length of Mexico, I have defeated a mad inventor, and I have lived with a lost tribe. If you are looking for a mere errand boy at some bargain price, I am not your man."

The three of them exchanged glances. Holzmann said, "Fine. Five."

"I have not yet agreed to your offer, Mr. Holzmann. I am merely clarifying the terms that you are offering."

"Very well, Derringer," Clement said. "Consider it clarified.

Are you interested?"

"There are other considerations besides the terms of the engagement, sir. *Why* do you think this task calls for an adventurer, rather than an ordinary search party?"

"It needn't require an adventurer," Mr. Murray replied. "After all, Smith said he did not consider himself an adventurer, and we only came to you because of Smith's unfortunate demise."

"Still, Mr. Beckwith-Smith was a resourceful man of unusual talents; why not simply hire a few idlers from the streets of Ogden?"

"Because we don't trust 'em!" Mr. Holzmann exclaimed.

"And what is there about this mission that requires an unusual degree of trust? You want to find a missing man; why all this mystery?"

Mr. Murray sighed. "I think we had somehow hoped not to tell you, but it appears it can't be avoided. Tell me, Mr. Derringer, what do you know about paleontology?"

That, I confess, caught me completely by surprise. I blinked. "Paleontology?" I asked. "The study of ancient life?"

"Yes."

I looked from one man to the other, utterly baffled as to what this had to do with Teddy Hancock. "I suppose I have a typical layman's knowledge, sir," I replied. "I am no expert in the field."

"Have you heard of the so-called 'Bone Wars' currently being waged in the mountains and plains of America?"

"I...am not certain what you are referring to." I glanced at the others, but they seemed content to leave the explanations to Mr. Murray.

"Have you ever heard of Professor Othniel Charles Marsh, formerly of Yale University?"

I admitted I had not.

"Or Mr. Edward Cope, of Pennsylvania?"

Again I confessed ignorance.

"These two men are the finest, most knowledgeable

paleontologists in America today. Each of them has added as much knowledge to the study of dinosaurs as the totality that had existed before their arrival in the field. Their discoveries have been astonishing."

I nodded.

"And they hate each other," Mr. Murray continued. "They absolutely *detest* one another. What began as a friendly rivalry has gotten completely out of hand. They are no longer working to expand the boundaries of science; now each strives only to demonstrate his superiority to the other, preferably by completely destroying the other man's reputation. Since dueling is out of fashion in modern academia, and since museums prefer not to support outright murder, both are still alive and working and competing in every way they can. Both these scientists employ dozens of fossil hunters, and will also bid competitively for finds made by amateurs; furthermore, several of their supposed employees have been found to also be working for the other man, resulting in more bidding wars. Both men seem to be devoting their entire fortunes to this competition."

"This is interesting and unfortunate," I said, "but I do not see how it is relevant."

"The point is," Mr. Clement said, "that they have brought about a huge increase in popular and academic interest in dinosaurs, and in combination with their frenzied bidding, this interest has driven the *price* of any significant new dinosaur finds to absurd levels. The skeleton of a long-dead lizard can bring hundreds of dollars from Cope or Marsh, or the various museums back East."

"Ah. And you think Teddy Hancock may have made such a discovery?"

"You think Hancock was a bone-digging prospector?" Mr. Holzmann said with a laugh, breaking his silence. "Nonsense! The man's an adventurer, like yourself."

"If I may continue?" Mr. Murray said.

"If you'll get to the confounded point," Mr. Holzmann retorted.

"Yes. Mr. Derringer, most of the major dinosaur finds in the American West to date have been in Nebraska, Colorado, and the Wyoming Territory, but some of the more ambitious fossil hunters have theorized there could be important fossil beds in the Utah Territory as well, and have begun collecting reports from the locals in hopes of selling news of some major site to Mr. Cope and Dr. Marsh. So far, no significant discoveries have been made, but last year rumors began to circulate in certain communities that a truly *astonishing* discovery had been made in the Wasatch Mountains, east of the Great Salt Lake - specifically, in the wilderness to the northeast of Ogden. I do not know whether these stories reached Mr. Cope or Dr. Marsh, but they most certainly *did* reach some members of the community of adventurers, including our missing Mr. Hancock."

"And Mr. Hancock went to investigate these rumors and this supposed discovery?"

"Exactly." Mr. Murray sat back in his chair, a satisfied expression on his face.

"We hired him to do it, and made sure to discourage any *other* adventurers from getting in his way," Mr. Holzmann said. I thought he sounded a little smug about it.

"We financed him," Mr. Murray said. "We did not *hire* him, as such."

"It's the same thing," Mr. Holzmann retorted.

I was not interested in hearing them bicker, and before Mr. Murray could respond I said, "I thought you said that Teddy was not just another prospector for bones. What made *these* bones so special that an adventurer was called upon?"

"Well, that's the thing, Mr. Derringer," Mr. Clement said. "It wasn't bones."

"Then what the devil *was* it?" I exclaimed. "What's this all about?"

"It wasn't bones," Mr. Murray said, echoing his companion. "It was dinosaurs. Real living, breathing dinosaurs."

I stared at him for a moment, half expecting one of the three to burst into laughter, but all of them seemed utterly serious.

"Dinosaurs have been extinct for millions of years," I said.

"Well, we can't really *know* that, can we, Mr. Derringer?" Mr. Holzmann replied. "We haven't searched the entire planet."

"That's right," Mr. Murray said. "We can't be *sure*. You, as an adventurer, know there are still many mysterious things in the world – ghosts, lost cities, and so on. Are a few stray dinosaurs, lingering long after their time in some unexplored corners, really so very unlikely?"

I looked from one to the next. "Gentlemen," I said, "if you were to tell me that a dinosaur had been glimpsed deep in the jungles of the Amazon, or in the unexplored heart of Africa, I would have my doubts, but I would not dismiss it out of hand. But in the Utah Territory? Yes, I know, I know, there are still vast swaths of the American hinterlands where no white man has set foot, but the *red* men have been everywhere, have they not? Would we not long since have heard tales of great beasts from the Indians, if there really were any such creatures roaming our country?"

"Would they have told us?" Mr. Clement asked. "If the dinosaurs were sacred to them, as so many of Nature's most wondrous creations are, might they not have held their tongues?"

I hesitated. I had just spent months among the Skyless, but for the most part the stories told aboveground had said that if the lizard people had ever existed, they were long dead. I had spoken with men who had visited Quivira, also known as El Dorado, the golden city most people believed to be a mere myth. I had seen metal brought out of the Lost City of the Mirage, and while no one denied that city's existence – there had been too many witnesses, too much accumulated evidence of its reality – its origin and nature were a mystery, and it appeared and vanished with no obvious pattern or logic.

My father, according to his journals, had visited legendary places and had seen astonishing creatures, often returning home with no proof of his adventures, yet I did not doubt the veracity of his accounts.

What if these dinosaurs were another such aberration? What if they had been sealed away somewhere for millions of years, and only now released, by some mechanism of which we were completely unaware? What if Mr. Clement's theory that the natives of the region had intentionally kept them secret was correct? I could not, in fairness, say that was completely absurd.

And this explained why this committee wanted an adventurer. This was what we *did* – confront, explain, and control the unknown, the inexplicable, and the uncontrollable.

"I'll need to know all the details," I said. "Everything the stories said, where the rumors originated, all of it."

"Then you'll do it?" Mr. Clement asked.

"Gentlemen, I will need more to go on than 'somewhere northeast of Ogden,' but if you can provide sufficient guidance to get me well begun on this quest, and if we can agree on the precise terms, then yes, I am willing to take the job. You have piqued my interest."

With that, Mr. Murray pulled a sheaf of paper from inside his jacket, and the real negotiations began.

Chapter Five

The Quest Begins

In the end, to Mr. Holzmann's extreme annoyance, we settled upon a fee of $600 for Teddy Hancock's safe return, and a one-eighth share in the net proceeds should the journey prove profitable, either through the discovery of actual living dinosaurs or through some serendipitous find such as a gold mine or an archeological treasure trove. Mr. Cartwright would provide assistance and certain minimal supplies, but any expenses beyond that were my own responsibility.

Mr. Murray had among his papers a copy of Peter Cartwright's notes about the rumors and reported sightings, including the headings and landmarks that Teddy Hancock was supposed to have been following, and this was turned over to me, though I assumed additional copies had been made and retained. Other potentially useful information, including two contradictory maps of the area east of Ogden, was also provided. In return I answered a few questions about my intentions, though most of those answers came down to, "It will depend on the circumstances I encounter." I did admit that Betsy might accompany me and would be told the nature of the expedition in any case; that brought more grumbling from Mr. Holzmann but was deemed unavoidable.

At last our business was concluded with handshakes all around, and my new employers departed. I gathered up the papers and took them up to my room for further study.

When the daylight started to fade, however, I did not light a lamp, but instead put aside everything to do with the job I had accepted, straightened my attire, and crossed the hall to knock on the door of Betsy's room.

She answered, and as we stood face to face in the doorway I was dreadfully tempted to kiss her, and from the expression on her face I had the distinct impression that she half expected me to and might not have objected. I controlled myself, though – this was not the proper time, nor the proper place. Instead I merely asked, "Would you care to join me for supper?"

"Did you take the job?" she asked.

"I did," I admitted. "I found it intriguing, and the pay is enough to justify some effort. I would be delighted to discuss it over a steak dinner, which I see is offered on today's menu downstairs."

"Then let us get such a dinner!" I had expected her to need a moment to freshen up, but she surprised me by stepping out into the hall and closing the door behind her. "Shall we go?"

We found our way once more to the American Dining Room and procured a relatively quiet table. The room could reportedly seat six hundred diners at a time, but on that particular evening it was scarcely half full, so we were able to find some privacy.

We placed our order, made some polite conversation, and then got down to business – specifically, the commission I had accepted. The discussion went smoothly until I explained what Mr. Hancock had been seeking, whereupon the smile vanished from Betsy's charming face, and she glared silently at me, frowning ferociously.

I gazed back with as open and honest a countenance as I could, and at last she said, "*Dinosaurs*, Tom? Really?"

"So they say," I replied. "It may well prove to be a misunderstanding, or an outright fraud, but that *is* what Teddy Hancock was after."

"And you're going to go looking for them?"

"Why, no," I said, genuinely startled. "I'm only looking for Mr. Hancock. *He* was looking for dinosaurs, and since he has disappeared, it seems likely that he found *something* in those hills, but whether it was dinosaurs or some far more ordinary menace – or for that matter, an even more bizarre one – I have as yet no opinion."

"And you won't go looking for the dinosaurs yourself?"

"I will be looking only for Teddy Hancock."

"And suppose you find him frozen to death on a mountain somewhere – then what?"

"I will bring his remains back to Ogden and deliver them to Mr. Cartwright. I will collect my pay – or at least two-thirds of it, the remainder being contingent upon bringing him back alive – and then I will go home."

"You won't go after the dinosaurs?"

"No, I will not."

"But you're an adventurer; surely, that is an adventure worth undertaking, just as much as seeking out the Phoenix airship or Gabriel Trask?"

I considered her point for a moment, not having previously given it a great deal of conscious thought. I had bought her father's flying machine and traveled halfway across the continent pursuing a mysterious object seen in the skies over the town of Phoenix on little more than a whim, and had come to California seeking the mysterious Mr. Trask simply as an excuse to take the two of us away from home for a time. Hunting for dinosaurs was no more absurd, and I finally said, "You are absolutely correct, as usual. It *is* an adventure worth undertaking. It is not, however, one I *want* to undertake. I cannot explain my reasoning in this, for honestly, I do not pretend to have reached this conclusion by reason at all; it simply does not interest me at the present time. I will look for Teddy Hancock because I found him congenial when we met on the train, and the committee is paying me to do so, but then I want to go home again before pursuing any further adventures. I do not even know what I would do with a dinosaur if I were to find one. I know...well, not nothing, but little about capturing big game, and it would be a shame to kill so rare a creature." I shook my head. "That is not a matter I wish to deal with. I only want to find Teddy Hancock. I would honestly prefer to *not* find any dinosaurs, but to discover merely that he lost his way, or ran afoul of a bear or mountain lion, or got himself trapped somewhere."

She stared at me, but just then the waiter brought our food, interrupting the conversation. When we had made our way through the customary details and had each eaten a little, Betsy put down her fork and said, "You surprise me, Tom Derringer. I would have thought a report of dinosaurs would have you eager to investigate."

I shrugged. "One cannot investigate *everything*," I said. "I did not coax Mr. Trask to take me to El Dorado, nor have I attempted to find the Lost City of the Mirage. I did nothing to interfere with the *status quo* in Chan Santa Cruz once McKee's airship was down. I have not taken ship to explore the jungles of Africa or the polar ice. I pursue only those matters that catch my fancy. Teddy Hancock's disappearance is such a matter, while reports of roaming Iguanodons are not."

Betsy cocked her head. "I believe Iguanodons were native to Europe, not North America," she said.

"Were they? I had no idea. I merely remembered hearing the name."

"It is not in those papers Mr. Murray gave you?"

"I don't believe so. Those describe..." I paused, trying to

recall the pompous names. "Hadrosaurus," I said, "and Stegosaurus, Allosaurus, and Brontosaurus – those are listed as the major varieties known in the American West, and the scientists who reported on the matter suggest that the alleged sightings best correspond to Stegosaurus and Brontosaurus."

"Well, that's just as well," Betsy said. "Those are both herbivores. I would not care to encounter a live Allosaurus under *any* circumstances; that appears to have been the fiercest of the ancient carnivores."

I stared at her. "How do you know that?" I asked.

"Really, Tom!" she said, with what appeared to be genuine affront. "My father is a scientist. I listened when he spoke. Admittedly paleontology is not his field, but he took an interest all the same and would read the newspaper accounts of the latest discoveries to my mother over supper. He greatly admired Dr. Marsh, but found Mr. Cope's discoveries somewhat suspect."

Astonished, I took a moment to gather my wits. "I did not have the privilege of dining with my father at an age when I could have understood such a discussion," I finally replied. "And I suspect he would have taken an interest in rather different parts of the news, in any case. I know almost nothing about dinosaurs. Now I find myself wondering whether *you* might want to go searching for them."

She shook her head. "I much prefer them to remain harmless fossils, to be marveled at in museums."

"That's fine, then," I said. "I would suggest that we use tomorrow to settle matters here in San Francisco, and head east the following day."

"To Ogden."

"Yes."

"Not New York."

"To Ogden."

She sighed. "Am I to share in the pay for this enterprise?"

"Of course!" I said. "You are still on my payroll as my

assistant, and that will not change until I deliver you safely back home." I did not specify whether I meant her home, or my own.

I also realized, having mentioned the subject, that I owed Betsy a significant amount of back pay; our expedition to California had lasted several months longer than intended. I had given her a share of the money Mr. Arbuthnot had sent, to cover her immediate expenses, but in fact it was not adequate to cover her promised salary for the time we had spent in and beneath Los Angeles, let alone for a new adventure in the Utah Territory.

"Very well. Now, if you will excuse me, I do not want my steak to get cold."

With that, we set to eating again, and further conversation was mere polite chit-chat, or planning out our actions for the next day.

When we had finished I had thought at first that we might retire to our rooms, but then inspiration struck. As we left the hotel's dining room, emerging into the lobby, I asked, "Would you care to go dancing, Miss Vanderhart?"

I had never seen Betsy look so shocked, but after no more than a second or two her expression of astonishment was transformed into a brilliant smile. "I do believe I would, Mr. Derringer!"

With that, I inquired of the concierge and was given directions to a nearby hall.

I would like to say that we did not embarrass ourselves, but that would be a greater untruth than I will allow myself in this narrative. Our mutual inexperience and the difference of perhaps ten inches in our heights made us awkward. I will say that we recovered ourselves after our various missteps, I did not ever quite tread on Betsy's feet, and all in all the evening was a success that brought us back to our hotel rooms well after midnight in a state of exhausted hilarity.

And on this occasion I did not resist temptation and Betsy did not resist my advance when I kissed her goodnight. It was a long and very satisfactory kiss, and it was only reluctantly that I released her and watched her vanish into her room. I was still quite giddy when I finally managed to undress and fall into my own bed.

Unsurprisingly, we slept later than I had intended, but I was still able to make the rounds, purchasing the items I thought we would need for the journey and stopping by the telegraph office to see whether there were any further messages from back East. While I did this Betsy spent a happy hour or so riding the cable cars and visiting one of the powerhouses, where she charmed her way inside to study the sheaves, cables, and other machinery; given her fondness for good engineering, the only surprise was that she had not done this sooner.

I did not purchase everything that we would need for hiking through northern Utah; I assumed I would be able to obtain much of it in Ogden. I did, however, buy a new Colt revolver; that was an item that would not take up a great deal of space, and there might be occasion for it before we reached Ogden.

After we had made the purchases I thought necessary, I let Betsy take the lead. She needed to further rebuild her wardrobe. We ate a late lunch at Martin & Horton's, a rather rough-and-tumble establishment that had been a favorite of the late Emperor Norton and that still drew several eccentrics. There we were regaled with tales of Black Bart, the mysterious stage-robbing poet who had finally been apprehended while we were in Los Angeles – it turned out that his real name was Charles Earl Boles, and until his capture he had been one of the regulars at Martin & Horton's.

After lunch I made an attempt to call on Ah How, the Chinese gentleman who had told us where to look for Gabriel Trask when we were first in San Francisco, but we were told he was out of town. Whether he was actually traveling, or his countrymen sought to protect him from me for some reason, I cannot be certain.

While we were in Chinatown I bought a few trinkets I thought my mother and sister might like, and then we continued our more mundane errands.

At last we returned to our hotel to drop off our purchases, then ventured out again for our supper. I thought about perhaps suggesting another dance, but my feet were sufficiently sore that I decided against it.

You might think that after that we would be ready to depart on the first ferry the next morning, but in fact we were not. Since Mr. Hancock had already been missing for months I saw no need to rush. There were arrangements to be made, wires to be sent, further discussion to be had with my new employers. I wanted to make sure my mother knew where we would be and so I told her, in both telegrams and letters, what details I could of the job I had accepted; the terms of my employment were such that I could give very few specifics. I was not to give her any names, or mention dinosaurs in any context whatsoever, so I merely said I had been hired to seek a lost adventurer in the mountains of the Utah Territory.

In addition to discussion of my new employment, I sent letters to Mr. Dobbs and Mr. Cartwright detailing the circumstances of Mr. Beckwith's death – or at any rate, those circumstances that I felt at liberty to reveal. I made no mention of Skyless lizard people, golden tablets, or tunnels beneath Los Angeles. I expected to meet Mr. Cartwright in person, but thought it best to fulfill my promise beforehand; if he had any further questions, I said, I would be happy to answer them when we met.

As for Mr. Dobbs, I said that I regretted not having an opportunity to meet him in person, but thought it more important to begin the job for which he and his fellows had hired me.

In addition to all those various tasks that had to be accomplished, I wanted to give Betsy's mother time to reply to her daughter's telegrams.

Besides, I had said I would be staying at least a week at the Palace and I intended to abide by that.

At last, though, everything was ready, and on Thursday, the

thirteenth of March, after a final telegram to Peter Cartwright to confirm our plans to meet with him in Ogden, we took the ferry across the bay to the railhead and boarded our eastbound train.

Betsy had still heard nothing from her parents. She had sent four telegrams in all, three addressed to her mother at home, and one to her father's office at Rutgers University. The last two had included our departure date and destination.

She had grown quieter and more downhearted with each passing day, and this continued even after we were on the train. She was not interested in conversation; instead we both spent most of the journey studying the papers Mr. Murray had given us. I hoped that reaching Ogden and venturing out into the wilderness might take her mind off the parental silence, but I could not in good conscience say that I *expected* it.

As our train made its stop in Sacramento I debated making an unplanned visit to Mr. Dobbs, to provide a fresh distraction, but I decided against it. I thought my letter would be sufficient to fulfill my promise to John Beckwith, and we stayed aboard the train.

It did not help Betsy's mood, nor my own, when we arrived in Ogden promptly on schedule at 8:00 a.m. on Saturday the fifteenth in pouring rain – the skies were gray from horizon to horizon, and the downpour was relentless. I had thought that we might find some lingering snow at that altitude and that far inland, as we had seen some in the mountains we had crossed, and all reports had been that the winter was a harsh one, but there was only mud and cold drenching rain. Even the hawkers who normally crowded the platform had been defeated by the torrent and were nowhere to be seen. We engaged a porter and headed down the boardwalk to the Reed Hotel.

Compared to our rooms at the Palace back in San Francisco the Reed seemed small and shabby; compared to the compartment we had shared for the two days on the train it was a palace in its own right, if a somewhat threadbare one. We took adjoining single rooms on the second floor, with a view of Wall

Street, and were able to change into dry clothing before meeting again in the lobby. We found seats near the fireplace to drive some of the cold and damp from our bodies and our souls.

I had originally thought that our early arrival would allow us to outfit ourselves completely on Saturday, so that we could meet with Mr. Cartwright on Saturday evening and set out into the Wasatch Mountains on Sunday morning. However, the rain and mud, combined with the fatigue brought on by our two days on the train, left neither of us in any mood to put forth the concerted effort such a scheme required. Instead we spent the morning at the Reed, conversing with the locals about the weather, what we might expect to find to the east, where we might find the equipage we sought, and other such topics.

After a pleasant if simple lunch I finally overcame my lethargy enough to set out into town in search of the supplies we would need, leaving Betsy at the hotel. We were still expecting Peter Cartwright to join us at the hotel after supper – our exchange of telegrams had not considered the weather as a reason to postpone – and I did not want him to think I had wasted the entire day. I added a new Winchester rifle and ammunition to our meager arsenal, as well as buying tents, blankets, and other basic equipment. My old Winchester, and most of our other supplies from previous purchases, had been lost somewhere in the tunnels under Los Angeles.

I also sent telegrams to both my mother and to Betsy's to let them both know we had come this far safely. I had some hope that Mrs. Vanderhart might respond to me, where she would not reply to her daughter. Only after the wires were sent did it occur to me that if she *did* answer me, informing Betsy might provoke more anger than gratitude.

By late afternoon the rain had subsided a little, and a few rays of sunshine managed to penetrate the overcast, illuminating the mountain slopes to the east. I looked at those and sighed.

Betsy had heretofore refused to ride horseback; in southern

California we had used a wagon or our own feet. Looking eastward, though, I was quite sure that no wagon would make it over those mountains. I would need a pair of mules, and Betsy could either ride one, or stay behind in Ogden.

I was not looking forward to telling her that.

Chapter Six

We Make Our Preparations

After we had eaten our supper Betsy and I were having a quiet but spirited argument in the lobby of our hotel about the necessity of riding mule-back when a voice said, "Tom Derringer, I presume?"

I turned and recognized the speaker immediately, even though I had only seen him at most twice before, months earlier – once right there at the Reed Hotel with Teddy Hancock and another man, and less certainly the following day among half a dozen men on the platform as our westbound train pulled out of the station. I had not gotten a good look at him among the latter group, but this was definitely the same man I had seen with Mr. Hancock. He was not quite my own height, clean-shaven, with a slender build and narrow jaw. He was wearing a stained Stetson hat and was carrying a large satchel.

I had not been introduced on that occasion, but I had little doubt who this was. "Mr. Cartwright?" I said, rising from my chair and offering my hand.

"Yes. A pleasure to meet you," he said, as we shook.

"I believe we met before, in this very spot," I replied.

He smiled crookedly. "I do recall that, but we did not speak on that occasion," he said. "I don't believe it counts as meeting someone if no one speaks."

"I suppose that's true. Would you care to join us, or shall we find somewhere more private to talk?"

"I think privacy might be wise."

"Then shall we retire to my room?"

He nodded, and the three of us walked up the hotel's grand staircase, such as it was, and down the corridor to my room. As we did Cartwright cast a curious glance at Betsy, and I made a belated introduction.

"Mr. Cartwright, this is my associate and confidant, Miss Elspeth Vanderhart. She will probably be accompanying me in my investigations. When you arrived, though, we were discussing a detail that might discourage her participation."

"Can't say I think those mountains are a fit place for a woman, Mr. Derringer."

I smiled. "I assure you, Miss Vanderhart is as capable as most men."

He looked at her, all five feet and an inch or so of her, with her blonde curls and lace collar, and did not seem convinced.

But then we were at my door, and I stood aside as Betsy and Mr. Cartwright stepped in, before following them and locking the door behind us. By the time I pocketed the key and turned around Mr. Cartwright had his satchel open and was pulling out papers, which he then spread on the bed.

These, I saw, were maps. They were similar to those Mr. Murray had provided in San Francisco.

"Teddy – Mr. Hancock – had copies of these," Mr. Cartwright said. "We had reports of sightings in *this* area." He spread his hand across one of the maps. "That's about fifty miles northeast of Huntsville."

"And where is Huntsville?"

He seemed startled; he looked up at me and said, "Fifteen miles east of here, just the other side of the ridge, in the Ogden

Valley."

I nodded. That agreed with one of the maps I already possessed and with some of the reports I had been given. "So that isn't all wilderness?"

"Not all of it, no. There are at least three communities in the Ogden Valley – Huntsville, Eden, and Liberty. We've been settling this area for some time now, Mr. Derringer."

"'We'?"

"The Latter-Day Saints."

"Ah," I said.

Up until that moment I had not realized that Mr. Cartwright was a Mormon; no one had seen fit to mention this to me. I suppose I should have guessed as much, though, given that he resided in Salt Lake City. Ogden, too, was largely Mormon, as was virtually the entire Utah Territory.

I did not suppose at the time that it mattered. The Mormons, or Latter-Day Saints as they preferred to be called, had largely made their peace with the rest of the United States, though I knew that the questions of polygamy and statehood were both vexed matters – the Mormons wanted to run their own affairs, while Congress was determined that their church should have no part in any government. I knew some of the issues still under dispute but had not paid close attention to the details, since until agreeing to search for Teddy Hancock I had not intended to spend much time in the Territory, but my understanding was that the disagreements were maintained with words and edicts at this point, rather than the violence that had characterized it a generation before.

The information Mr. Murray had provided made no mention of the Latter-Day Saints; presumably he had not thought it relevant to our quest.

"We know of eight, possibly nine sightings, all in this area," Mr. Cartwright continued. "Most were of lone monsters, glimpsed at a distance, but one reported seeing two of the creatures." He pulled more papers from his satchel. "These are some sketches based on those reports."

I looked at the crude drawings, which depicted humpbacked things with some sort of spikes or fins along the spine. I had already seen tracings of these, though Cartwright's were more detailed, and I knew that these were thought to be Stegosaurus. Or perhaps the plural would be Stegosauri, or Stegosauruses; I had never bothered to get that straight.

The one sighting of another variety had produced a rather different sketch, of a thing resembling a long-necked wingless dragon. That, I had been told, was a Brontosaurus.

Neither was anything I particularly wanted to see first hand. I supposed that the estimates of their size were terrifically exaggerated, and Betsy had assured me that both species were as herbivorous as horses, but even so the idea of meeting these monsters still held little appeal.

But then, I had not been hired to find dinosaurs. "You think Mr. Hancock headed that way? That he was following the landmarks in these notes?"

"We do. If not, we have no idea where he went."

I nodded. "He was on horseback?"

"I believe he was."

"Alone?"

"Yes." Mr. Cartwright frowned. "He insisted on going alone; we had argued about it, in fact. I had wanted to send a small party under his direction, perhaps even go along myself, but he said he'd do better on his own. Said he'd be able to do things his own way and not worry about some bumbling amateur warning off his quarry, if he were by himself."

"And he wouldn't have to share his discoveries."

"He never said that, but I reckon it's the truth."

"Adventurers need to be very careful whom they trust, Mr. Cartwright."

"I'm sure you do."

"So he rode off alone. You don't know anything about his mount? Or what supplies he took?"

"No. We left that to him."

"All right. You wouldn't happen to have a photograph of Teddy Hancock, would you?"

He started. "What do you want a picture for? You've met him!"

"But I may want to talk to people I meet on the way."

"Well, I don't have a photograph, don't think anyone does, so you'll just need to do without."

"Very well." A photograph, or even just a drawing, might have been helpful, but I thought I could manage without one. Or perhaps I could have one sent from the Pierce Archives in New York – but that would take too long. "What else can you tell me?"

"Blessed little, I'm afraid. Mr. Hancock had the same maps and reports we've given you. He set out into the hills in late September and wasn't ever seen again."

"And when did the first snows fall?"

"I don't recall exactly; earlier than usual, I think. Probably some time in October."

"Could he have holed up somewhere for the winter?"

"We reckon he likely did exactly that. He meant to return before the snows came, but maybe he misjudged, or maybe he reconsidered."

I frowned. "It's only March."

Cartwright nodded.

"I'm not sure why you hired me this soon, rather than waiting to see whether he might yet return."

"Because if he did hole up somewhere, we still would have expected him back weeks ago. It's been a *cold* winter, but it wasn't a particularly snowy one, not for folks around here. Under normal circumstances he could have made it back out of the mountains by now."

I remembered that Mr. Murray had told us that he and his friends had only resolved to send someone after Teddy Hancock a few days before I had arrived in San Francisco. "You do not think you may have been hasty?"

Mr. Cartwright grimaced. "Mr. Derringer," he said, "I know Teddy. I've known him for three years now, ever since business took me to Chicago and we ran into one another there. I *like* Teddy. He is a fearless and stubborn man, and I think that if he could have returned by now, he would have. I considered going after him myself, and if you hadn't turned up when you did I might well have done it. In fact, I would be glad to accompany you, if you would allow it."

That was not a possibility anyone had mentioned heretofore. I glanced at Betsy. She spread her hands wordlessly, clearly as surprised as I was.

"Your partners never discussed such an option," I said.

"I hadn't really talked to them about it. *They* weren't about to do anything they thought was dangerous."

"You agreed with them to hire me, did you not?"

"Yes, I did, because you are an adventurer, and I am not – I'm just a businessman. I think you have a better chance of finding Teddy and bringing him back safely than I would. Until this very moment I had intended to let you operate as you thought best, and in fact that is still my intention, but I wanted to let you know that *if you think it best*, I am ready to join your expedition."

"Are you comfortable on a mule's back?" I tried not to look at Betsy as I asked this.

"I'm more familiar with horses, but I think I could manage well enough."

"You don't have anything keeping you here in town, or back in Salt Lake? A wife or family, or business concerns?"

He hesitated. "I don't have a wife, but business... How long do you expect to be gone?"

"Well, that's the thing about adventuring, Mr. Cartwright," I said. "You never really know. Mr. Murray said you had expected Mr. Hancock back by Christmas, and I had thought that I'd be back East with my family by Christmas, but here we are, three months later, and I'm in Ogden instead of New York, and we don't know where Mr. Hancock is."

"Of course." He considered for a long moment, then said, "Do you think I'd be a help to you, Mr. Derringer, or a nuisance?"

"I can't really say with any certainty, Mr. Cartwright, but right now I think you know this country better than I do, and you know the people around here better than I do, and you know Teddy Hancock better than I do, and all that knowledge might prove useful. Yes, you may well lack in other areas, and I'm not ruling out sending you back home by yourself if you do turn out to be a nuisance, but if you want to come along, I'd welcome your company." I smiled. "And Miss Vanderhart's mother might find it reassuring to know that we have a chaperone."

Betsy snorted. "I think it's a little late for that to matter."

"It can't do any harm," I replied.

"Then...when do we leave?" Cartwright asked.

"If we can assemble all the supplies we need, I would be glad to depart first thing in the morning."

"I think I can probably make sure you have whatever you think you'll want. Shall we make a list?"

I nodded and pulled out a piece of paper. "First, we'll need three...no, four mules – one for each of us, and one for our gear. With any luck, Teddy Hancock will wind up riding that fourth one, and we'll divide up whatever else we may have to carry."

Mr. Cartwright nodded. Then he frowned. "I don't know that I can find those on a Sunday. We take the Sabbath seriously around here. And I'm not about to buy livestock in the dark, so I can't get them tonight."

I was not surprised to hear this. "You don't happen to own any?"

"I do not. I have a horse tied outside; I've never owned a mule."

I glanced at Betsy. "I would really prefer mules for this expedition. I believe they would be more suited to the terrain."

"I'll yield to your expertise, Mr. Derringer, but in that case I don't think we'll be able to leave until at least Monday."

"Tuesday," Betsy volunteered, startling us both. "We'll need some time to get everything loaded. But we should be able to head out first thing Tuesday morning."

Mr. Cartwright looked at her, then back at me, and saw that I was giving no indication I disagreed or intended to overrule my companion. "I'm disappointed it can't be sooner," he said, "but again, I'll defer to your experience, if you're sure."

"The delay might not be strictly necessary," I said, "but I do think it wiser not to rush our preparations. Will you be available tomorrow, to help us prepare? I won't ask you to break the Sabbath if it troubles you."

"I appreciate that, Mr. Derringer. I would prefer not to work on a Sunday, and some of the supplies we want may not be available. Shall we meet on Monday morning, then?"

"Monday it is."

Then he rose, and we shook hands. Betsy and I accompanied him back down to the hotel lobby and saw him on his way.

The moment the door closed behind him Betsy turned and glowered at me. "*Must* it be mules?"

"They are, as I was saying, easier and more comfortable for a beginner than horses," I replied, continuing the discussion Mr. Cartwright had interrupted. "More sure-footed in the mountains, more intelligent – "

"And notoriously stubborn and uncooperative!"

"You can ride a mule, or you can stay here in Ogden. Or if you prefer to return to New Brunswick, I will pay your train fare. But we are not going into those mountains on foot, or on wheels."

She glared silently at me a moment longer, and I took the opportunity to ask, "Why Tuesday? I think we could get half a day's travel in on Monday even if we can't do anything tomorrow."

"Because of your confounded *mules*!" she cried, throwing up her hands. "I want a day to learn how to ride one before I go off into the wilderness!"

"Ah," I said. "I think that's very wise."

She did not reply.

Chapter Seven

Into the Hills

We gathered at the stable by lantern-light, half an hour before Tuesday's dawn, and loaded our supplies and equipment onto the four fine mules that Mr. Cartwright had provided. Betsy was only slightly reluctant; her lessons in mule riding, carefully concealed from our fellow traveler, had gone well. She admitted that riding a mule was indeed more comfortable and less terrifying than perching atop a spirited horse, though she still did not enjoy it, and we had arranged for her to take the smallest and least intimidating of the four.

We had stopped by the local telegraph office and had sent our respective mothers reassuring messages, but had received no reply as of suppertime on Monday.

Fortunately, the rains had ceased for the most part on Sunday afternoon, and Monday had been dry, as well. That had allowed Betsy's riding practice to be done more comfortably, and there was every indication that Tuesday's skies would also be clear.

As the eastern sky lightened, even before the sun cleared the mountains, we set out, making our way through the streets of Ogden. By mid-morning, when we took our first real break, we were out of the city and well up the canyon road into the mountains.

We did not encounter anyone else on our journey. Had Mr. Cartwright not assured me otherwise, I might almost have thought we were already beyond the bounds of civilization and into the wilderness. A good-sized stream paralleled the road and provided water for the mules and ourselves whenever we paused to rest our mounts. Although the ground had a grayish color that I thought gave it an unhealthy appearance for much of the way, trees and grass lined the route, though it was too early in the spring for the trees to have leafed out, and the grass was still more brown than green. The slopes we could see above the trees on either side were largely bare stone, too steep or too hard to hold soil.

It was not a difficult ride. The weather was cold enough that whenever we stopped we would pull our coats tighter and stamp our feet to keep the blood flowing, but the sun shone through the clouds, it did not rain or snow, and the terrain was not so difficult as to trouble our mules.

We reached Huntsville early in the afternoon, sooner than I had expected. I think the mules had been hurrying, to keep themselves warm. At any rate, after some discussion we simply rode on, past the town and its surrounding farms, and on across the Ogden Valley toward the mountains to the east. There was nothing of any particular interest about the settlement, and it seemed unlikely anyone there would have anything to tell us of Teddy Hancock; Mr. Cartwright assured us that he had sent word to Huntsville, Eden, and Liberty weeks ago that he would pay for any news of his lost friend, but no reports had arrived.

We pressed on until sunset and made camp at the mouth of what Mr. Cartwright and our maps told us was Kelley Canyon, not far from a farm that may well have belonged to the Kelley family.

On Wednesday we made our way up the canyon, and from that point on we really *had* left civilization behind. We were following the route that we thought Mr. Hancock would most probably have taken, but in truth that was little more than guesswork.

We traveled more slowly now, not merely because there were no roads, but because we were looking for any evidence that our quarry might have come this way. Alas, that we had not begun our pursuit until months after his disappearance! We had virtually no chance of finding footprints or hoofprints after so long. Abandoned campsites might still leave traces even after an entire winter, but anything less than that would probably be completely gone.

We stopped frequently to investigate likely places – sheltered spots where he might have stayed overnight, or areas where a stream was especially convenient, or other such locations. We zigzagged our way up the canyon, sometimes venturing up one side or the other.

It began to rain again Wednesday night, and except for a few brief interruptions it did not stop until midday Friday.

We ate our evening meals around a campfire, and right from the first, on Tuesday night, Betsy took the opportunity to chat with Mr. Cartwright - or perhaps "gossip" would be the more correct, if less flattering, term. I had noticed before, in Mexico and in the tunnels of the Skyless, that she often seemed to know more than I about the people around us, and now I had the opportunity to see how she accomplished this. She would start off with some harmless comment about our surroundings, and then gradually work the conversation to more personal matters.

She asked about the other members of the committee that had hired us, beginning with the most harmless questions and then prompting for more details without ever seeming to pry. Thus we learned that Mr. Murray was happily married, with four adorable children; Mr. Dobbs, whom we had not met, was likewise domestically blessed with a charming wife and three daughters, the eldest of whom was starting to attract suitors. None of the other three were so fortunate. Mr. Holzmann's wife had left him and gone back East, and an exchange of bitter and accusatory letters had been going between them for the last few years. Mr. Clement's wife had died not long ago, and he gave no sign as yet of finding another.

As for Mr. Cartwright himself, he dismissed the question with a shrug. "I have yet to meet a member of the fair sex who suits my fancy," he said.

To my surprise, Betsy did not pursue the matter further.

On Wednesday the dinnertime inquisition began with a query about how Mr. Cartwright had come to meet Teddy Hancock, and then led into detailed questions about just what sort of a man we were searching for.

"Why is he called Steady Teddy?" she asked.

"Because in a tight situation he's steady as a rock," Mr. Cartwright replied. "The man is absolutely fearless in an open confrontation; he won't break, won't turn aside, won't back down."

"I wonder he has lived this long, then," I ventured.

"Well, that's another thing about him, Mr. Derringer," Mr. Cartwright said. "He *knows* that his sort of fearlessness can get a man killed, and so he has quite deliberately tempered it with caution. He always looks before he leaps, so to speak."

"He doesn't go looking for trouble?" Betsy asked.

Mr. Cartwright shook his head. "Never. But if trouble comes looking for *him*, he'll...well, I was going to say he'd meet it head-on, but that's not quite how it is. He'll look for a way to avoid it. But if he can't, *then* he'll meet it head on, without hesitation."

"He sounds like a good man to have at your side."

"I'd say he is," Mr. Cartwright agreed.

"How is it I haven't heard more about his adventures?"

"Oh, well, there are a few things."

"What do you mean?"

"Well, he's not the cleverest man in the world. I don't mean he's stupid, by any means; he's not. But the sort of inspired stratagem that might get an adventurer through a tricky situation doesn't come naturally to him. He's not noted for his wit or charm, either; for my own part I like his style, blunt though it may be, but I understand that others might not. He's more suited to working as part of a team than to leading one." He hesitated. "And then there's his stubborn streak."

"Oh?"

Mr. Cartwright sighed. "When Teddy sets his mind on something, there's no changing it. He's about as tenacious as a man can be. I suppose it goes with his fearlessness."

Betsy nodded. "If he works better as part of a team, why did he come out here alone?"

"Well, there are two parts to that. The first is that he's tired of living in the shadows of his more famous companions, and wanted to make a name for himself. And the second is that we *asked* him to."

"We?"

"The committee." He sighed again. "We wanted to keep this dinosaur business quiet, so the fewer who knew about it, the better. I knew Teddy from my stay in Chicago, and I suggested him to my partners as a man who can keep his mouth shut, and they agreed – but they wanted to hire *one* adventurer, not a team. Abbie Holzmann in particular wasn't keen on sending more than one. He'd already been paying adventurers *not* to go looking for dinosaurs, sending them off on other errands to keep them away from here. We've been doing everything we could to discourage anyone else from following up on the stories, and Holzmann and Dobbs didn't want to take any chances that someone on a team might go talking too much, or that the members might fight amongst themselves and draw attention. So we hired Teddy, and only Teddy."

I got the distinct impression that Mr. Cartwright regretted this choice.

The conversation rambled on, and on Thursday we learned a

little more about Mr. Cartwright's own background, but nothing I found of any great interest. He had been a resident of Salt Lake City since boyhood, and although he had visited half a dozen other cities in the course of his business he had little to say about any of them.

The product of our first three days of searching was one circular group of rocks that might have once surrounded a campfire, a depression that did not appear to be entirely natural, and several charred wood fragments that might have been the result of a lightning strike, or of a cookfire. We could not say with certainty how long any of these had been there. The stone ring might well have been there for decades, and the shallow pit could have been there for years.

As we made camp on Friday evening Betsy said, "Tom, this is ridiculous."

I looked up from driving a tent peg. "What is ridiculous?" I asked.

"This searching!" She waved a hand at the surrounding landscape. "How are we supposed to find one man in all this wilderness?"

I sat back on my heels. "Well," I said, "we do have some idea where he was heading. We know he won't go too far from water, and his original supply of food must have run out months ago, so he'll need sources of game and won't venture too far up toward the peaks. We can safely assume that he'll want to cook what he catches, and even the most expert woodsman - which, as I understand it, Teddy Hancock was not - cannot build a completely smokeless fire. I admit that spotting smoke in the dark, or in the rain, is not practical, but on sunny days we may well see it."

"And if he only builds a fire at night?"

"Then we may spot the glow."

"Maybe if we made our own camp on a mountaintop, we could."

"Well, we may just try that. At present I doubt we are close enough; we are trying to pick up a very cold trail."

"Tom, he might be long dead. Suppose he tried to shelter from the snow in a cave and disturbed a bear."

"Mr. Hancock is an experienced adventurer and a sensible man - as Mr. Cartwright explained the other night, he did not acquire the nickname 'Steady Teddy' by being careless. I assume he would have a gun in hand when he ventured into an unfamiliar cave, and that it would most probably be the bear that died, rather than Mr. Hancock."

From the corner of my eye I saw Mr. Cartwright shudder. I turned to him.

"She does have a point, though, Mr. Cartwright," I said. "While I think Teddy Hancock could probably handle a bear or two under normal circumstances, he could have died in any number of other ways - a fall or a fever, for example. If that happened and he is indeed dead, it may not be possible to locate his remains."

"I know, Mr. Derringer," he said, pulling his jacket tighter. "But I'm hoping for the best."

I nodded. "As am I. I wouldn't have taken this job if I thought I had no chance of success. But I admit that if we do not find some trace of his passage within a month or so, I may well abandon the hunt as hopeless. Back in San Francisco, or even in Ogden, the extent and emptiness of this wilderness was easier to underestimate."

"I'm sure it was. But it isn't infinite, Mr. Derringer, and Teddy *was* looking for something specific."

"Dinosaurs."

"Exactly."

I sighed. "I haven't seen any sign of *them*, either. Jackrabbits and mule deer, yes, and I thought I saw a cougar's paw mark in the mud by the stream yesterday, but nothing that could possibly indicate something the size of a dinosaur might be lurking nearby."

"But we know where they were sighted!"

"Within a substantial margin of error, yes, and we will do our best to pick up Mr. Hancock's trail there, Mr. Cartwright. I could use the money your partners offered – and if we do find dinosaurs along with Mr. Hancock, I have been promised a share of the proceeds from *that*, as well. I am not giving up; I am merely acknowledging that Miss Vanderhart may be right in suggesting that the task is beyond our capabilities and that poor Mr. Hancock may well be dead."

"Hmph."

That ended the discussion for a time, but later, when Betsy and I were seated by our campfire while Mr. Cartwright attended to certain personal business elsewhere, she said quietly, "You intend to stay out here in these mountains for a month?"

"Assuming we don't find Teddy, yes, I thought that would be a reasonable time to devote to our search. Do you disagree?"

"Now that I've seen this country, I think it's a fool's errand, and *any* time devoted to it is a waste!"

"Are you so eager, then, to return to your mother's care?"

She froze at that, staring at me without speaking for a moment, then said, "Is that what we're doing?"

I shrugged. "Well, I would be very happy to find Mr. Hancock alive and well and to earn the fee Mr. Cartwright's committee offered me, but yes, we are, in part, providing you with an excuse to stay away from the parental hearth a little longer. If you feel ready to face your mother I might be swayed to abandon our quest more quickly – or if you wish, I could extend it." I stretched and gestured at the scrubby trees around us. "And meanwhile, we can enjoy the fresh air and scenery."

The truth was that when I first accepted the committee's offer of employment I had thought finding Teddy Hancock might not be very difficult at all, since I did not think he had any reason to hide and might well be trying to attract rescuers by leaving messages or with signal fires. It was only later, when our telegrams

to Mrs. Vanderhart remained unanswered, that I realized this
venture might provide Betsy time to prepare her heart and mind
for reunion with her mother.

I still thought it very possible that we would indeed locate the
missing adventurer, but I knew it was far from certain, and I did
not want to get Mr. Cartwright's hopes too high.

Before either of us could say anything more that gentleman
returned, and we decided to restrict ourselves to the most
harmless of small talk.

Shortly after we retired to our respective tents that night the
rains returned, and they continued to fall, with only occasional
interruptions, thereafter.

Another four wet and dreary days brought us to what our
reports indicated as the very center of saurian activity, and I began
looking in earnest for campsites, messages, or traces of smoke – or
evidence of dinosaurs, such as tracks or leavings. I did not
immediately find any of those. The rain did not help in that
regard. Quite aside from the reduced visibility and the high
probability that evidence might have been washed away, almost
everything we had brought with us was now soggy, and the mules
were reluctant to come out from beneath the sheltering trees.

We found a rocky cliff that gave us a good vantage point to
look out over a fairly broad area to the east and south, but the
clouds and mist were such that we could not be sure of seeing all
there was to see. I was reluctant to abandon this perch until we
had a chance to use it in sunny weather, but simply sitting up there
did not seem like a good use of our time, so instead we made our
way down around the south end and began exploring along the
foot of the cliff. I thought it might have provided our quarry with
shelter at some point, and it was with moderate excitement that I
made out what appeared to be a trail or path at the base of the
stone barrier. There were even signs that campfires had been
buried here and there, though none appeared to be of recent
vintage, and I had no way of knowing whether they were the doing

of Teddy Hancock, or local settlers, or passing Indians. Betsy, Mr. Cartwright, and I all started investigating the various cracks and crevices where things might have been hidden – messages intended for Teddy's friends, supplies cached for later use, or other things entirely.

This was a time-consuming task, and we were still at it on Thursday night when the light above the cliff began to fade. We resolved to make camp in a depression beneath a rocky overhang, sheltered from rain and wind; we would continue our studies when Friday's dawn came. We did not pitch tents, since the stone protected us, but we did improvise canvas walls to keep out blowing rain, to shield us from passing predators, and to provide some privacy.

I was asleep in my bedroll behind that canvas drape when I was awakened by a faint hiss. I sat up abruptly and looked around at the darkness, thinking perhaps a snake had gotten into my shelter, or had been there all along and resented our intrusion on its home.

I could not see anything, and as I tried to remember the sound, in hopes of getting a better idea of its location, I realized it had not sounded much like a snake at all. What it *did* resemble I could not say; nothing like it came to mind.

I reached out in the gloom and pushed aside the canvas, but the darkness outside my little compartment was nearly as complete as within. I could see almost nothing, just slight variations in the blackness and a faint sense of movement from the falling rain.

I heard another hiss, this time without the intervening canvas, and realized that it was not coming from anywhere close at hand, but from somewhere at a considerable distance. The fact that it was audible over the steady patter of the rain made this all the more impressive; I realized it must have been loud. This, not proximity, was probably why it had awakened me so immediately.

"Tom!" Betsy's voice called, in a loud whisper. "Did you hear that?"

"I did," I acknowledged.

"What *was* that?"

"I have no idea," I whispered back. "Hush!"

She did not reply, and I eased myself out of my shelter, listening intently, trying to ignore the rain. I reached back and found my hat; I clapped it on my head, then groped in my pack for my Winchester.

Now the mules were awake, as well; I could hear them shuffling their feet. One snorted quietly.

"What's going on?" Mr. Cartwright asked, peering out from his own shelter.

"Shh!" Betsy replied.

Another hiss sounded. I crept forward, peering into the gloom, but could not make out much of anything. I knew the moon was just past full, but it was so thoroughly obscured by clouds that I could see no sign of its light – or perhaps it had set; I had no clear idea of the time. I hesitated, tempted to make my way toward the sounds, but aware that I might well become disoriented and become lost in the darkness, or walk into a tree or some other obstacle, or tumble down an unseen slope. In any case, I would probably make enough noise to warn whatever I sought; I had trained in moving silently in the woods, but never in such complete darkness and rain.

"What *is* that?" Mr. Cartwright whispered.

"I don't know," I said. I bit my lip and stared into the darkness, but my eyes could adjust no further. I took one step, and the rustling of wet leaves underfoot convinced me that in these conditions silence was probably impossible. I took another step, much more slowly, putting into practice what I had been taught of stealthy movement in forests, and managed to reduce the sound to a fraction of the first.

I listened again, but now I could hear nothing but the rain. I waited for what I judged to be several minutes, with my rifle at the ready, then said, "I think it's gone." Reluctantly, I retreated back into my shelter under the overhang. "We'll investigate in the morning. There's nothing more we can do right now."

I heard my companions moving about and heard their own canvas drapes falling back into place before I lowered my own. Warily, I settled back onto my bedding, setting the rifle down at my side, close at hand.

And then I pretended to sleep, but in truth I lay awake listening.

Chapter Eight

A Startling Discovery

I do not know how long I lay there, but at last the eastern sky lightened enough for a dull gray dawn to illuminate my canvas wall, letting me know that I need no longer feign sleep. I rose from my bedding and pulled down the cloth barrier that had shielded me.

The rain had dwindled to a cold mist, so that even with the faint light of morning I could still see no more than a few yards in any direction. As I folded my tent I could see that both my companions' shelters were still in place; a rivulet was dripping from the cliff above and trickling down across Betsy's canvas drape. I debated whether to be as quiet as I could, so that they might sleep, or whether to deliberately make enough noise to wake them, and decided on the former, as there was no need to be rude.

I slung my rifle on my back, rather than stowing it again, and buckled my gun belt around my waist with my new pistol in its holster; whatever we had heard last night might be nearby and dangerous. I gathered the rest of my gear, and then turned my attention to the mules. I was relieved to see that all four were still tethered to the trees where we had left them, all awake and alert. I set to currying them, murmuring comforting nonsense as I did.

I was brushing the smallest, Betsy's mount, when Betsy herself pushed aside a flap and emerged from her niche.

"Good morning," she said. She glanced at Mr. Cartwright's undisturbed tent, then reached up and began removing the wedged-in stones that supported her own.

A few minutes later we had cleared away much of our encampment and were debating whether to start a fire to cook breakfast or whether to wake Mr. Cartwright first, when a cough from behind the final canvas rendered the point moot. A few minutes later the three of us were gathered around a small fire, trying to fight off the chill of the cold, wet night.

"What do you suppose that was that we heard last night, Mr. Derringer?" Mr. Cartwright asked.

"I don't know," I said. "I'd like to investigate."

"Investigate *how?*" Cartwright asked.

"I have an idea of the direction it came from," I said, carefully doing nothing to indicate what that idea might be. I turned to Betsy. "Where would *you* judge it to be?"

As I had hoped, she pointed to the northeast – the same direction I had guessed. "We'll go that way, then," I said.

"Why?" Cartwright asked. "I would think we would want to stay *away* from whatever we heard."

"Mr. Cartwright," I said patiently, "we are in search of a lost adventurer. As an adventurer myself, I can say with some authority that it is in the nature of our mutual occupation to head *toward* danger or the unknown. If Mr. Hancock passed through this area and heard the sort of hissing we heard last night, I am morally certain he would have gone to investigate it. He might well have thought it to be made by the dinosaurs he sought, but even if he did not, he would have attempted to identify the source. Therefore, we should do the same."

"He probably *would* have thought it was dinosaurs," Betsy said.

"For all I know, it *was* dinosaurs," I replied.

Cartwright did not appear convinced, but an hour or so later, when we had eaten, broken camp, and attended to the other usual needs, we mounted our mules and set out in the direction whence we judged the hissing to have come.

We soon found ourselves following that faint path we had spotted the previous day – a path that was no longer quite as faint. This was, at the very least, a trail used by the local wildlife. I pointed this out to the others, and suggested that we should proceed with great caution. I was happy to see that the rain had stopped completely, at least for the moment, and it looked as if the sun might even, in time, break through the clouds.

I was watching ahead, in case of ambush or other such hazards, so it was Betsy, riding behind me, who first noticed the tracks.

"Tom," she called, "what sort of marks are those?"

I turned to see her pointing at the ground. I stopped my mount and looked down.

There were faint indentations in the path. I dismounted for a closer look, and both my companions followed my example.

They were not very deep; despite the rain the ground here had not been particularly muddy. The soil was mostly rock and sand, not conducive to taking clear impressions. Still, we could see the general outline, and more particularly, the *size*.

They were gigantic footprints, of a kind I had never seen before.

Mr. Cartwright was the first to break the silence.

"Looks to me," he said, "as if those stories about dinosaurs have something to them."

"They might, at that," I agreed.

There were imprints of at least two different sizes, as if either two creatures had made them, or one creature with differing fore and hind feet. They were not particularly fresh nor clear and seemed to be layered over one another, so we could not be sure how recent they were, or how many animals were responsible for them.

Something about them did not seem quite right to me, but I could not then say just what it was.

There was another peculiar feature accompanying the footprints – a shallow groove in the earth, several inches wide but less than an inch deep, ran down the center of the path. For a moment I thought it might indicate a channel where rainwater had drained away, but now I realized that was impossible. It rose and fell with the path, and water does not run uphill. Nor could it be the track of a wagon wheel of any variety I had ever encountered; it was too wide and slightly deeper in the center than at the sides.

"Look at this," Betsy said, pointing to this feature I had been observing.

"Something dragged there," Mr. Cartwright said.

"Its tail," Betsy said. She looked up at me. "Some dinosaurs are thought to have dragged their tails on the ground."

"Then you think we might be dealing with living dinosaurs after all?" I asked. "I thought you considered that idea absurd."

"I did," she said. "So did you. But absurd things happen sometimes."

I decided not to say anything more about the matter just then; instead I said, "Let's get moving."

We remounted and urged the mules forward.

The path led into a stand of aspen trees, and rocky slopes rose on either side of us; we were riding into a canyon or gorge, one that was not on our sketchy maps of the area, so although the clouds did finally part, revealing the morning sun, we remained largely in the shade. I was in the lead, and in the interests of caution I reduced my pace, advancing slowly. The path turned a corner ahead, I could see as much, but I could not see *around* the corner at all until we were almost upon it.

And then we reached the turn, where the path veered to the left and sloped sharply downward, and I found myself looking at a tall wooden stockade and a barred gate some thirty or forty yards ahead. I stopped, and leaned forward across the mule's neck, peering at this unexpected barrier. The wood was not freshly cut, by any means, but neither was it particularly weathered. I was not familiar enough with the local climate to assign an exact age, but I estimated it to be no more than a few years old.

I could hear the others coming up behind me, and then Mr. Cartwright exclaimed, "What the devil is *that?*"

Betsy shushed him; I glanced back to see her hand on his arm and a ferocious glare on her face.

"That's a very good question," I murmured far more quietly in response. I tugged on my reins, turning my mule around. "I think we had better get out of sight."

"Get out of *whose* sight?" Cartwright demanded. Betsy yanked at his arm so hard he almost tumbled from his saddle; startled, he turned to see her holding a finger to her lips. Without a word she released her grip on him, then turned her own mount around; the two of us rode back up and around the bend in silence, our pack mule close behind.

A moment later Mr. Cartwright joined us.

"I don't understand," he whispered, having finally grasped the need to lower his voice. "What *is* that place? I don't remember anything showing up on the map right around here."

"There *isn't* anything on the map," I replied. "Didn't you see that thing is in a box canyon, hidden from everyone?"

"But who...?"

"We *don't know*, you idiot," Betsy said. "But from how it's hidden away like that, whoever it is doesn't want company."

"We're lucky they didn't have sentries posted," I said.

"*If* they didn't," Betsy answered. "Maybe they're watching us right now, trying to figure out who *we* are."

At that suggestion I took an involuntary look around. There

was no one lurking in the trees around us, I was sure, nor on the path ahead or behind, but I had a definite impression that *something* was not right.

"I think we should get off the trail," I said.

Betsy nodded. Mr. Cartwright started to say something, then saw Betsy's expression and decided to hold his peace.

I led our little party past a thicket, then around an outcropping and other obstacles, into a bend in the side of the canyon where I was fairly certain we could not be seen from the path we had followed. There we dismounted and tied our mounts to a bush, then settled to the ground a few yards away to discuss our situation.

"All right," I said, shifting slightly in a futile attempt to find a drier spot to sit, "what's our next step? I was thinking that maybe we should circle around that enclosure, take a look at it from the other side, if we can."

Betsy said, "If there are people in there, we might be seen."

"If? You think it might be deserted?"

She shrugged.

"If you two are so sure we aren't welcome here, why don't we just leave it alone?" Mr. Cartwright asked.

"Because we're here to find Teddy Hancock," I said. "It's entirely possible he's behind that barrier."

"Why would he be in there?"

I stared at him in disbelief.

He noticed my expression. "I don't understand any of this," he complained. "We're looking for Teddy, and he's looking for dinosaurs, so he might have seen the trail we followed, but what does any of that have to do with some hidden fort?"

"Mr. Cartwright, whatever made those tracks appears to have gone through the gate we saw, and the sounds we followed almost certainly came from beyond it," I said. "Whatever is responsible for the tracks is probably responsible for the reports of dinosaurs, as well, and it's probably behind that stockade right now. Teddy

Hancock came here looking for dinosaurs; he may well have found that place, just as we have, and followed those tracks, or whatever made them, into the enclosure. He wouldn't have just turned away without investigating whatever is on the other side of that gate – not Steady Teddy! I don't know what that place is, or who is in there, but I think it likely that whoever built it would not welcome intruders. You don't hide away in an uncharted canyon and build a wall like that if you're looking forward to neighborly visits. If Mr. Hancock *did* get in there he may be dead, or being held prisoner, but I doubt he's being treated as an honored guest, free to leave when he pleases."

"Or he could be somewhere else entirely!" Mr. Cartwright insisted.

"Why would he be?" Betsy demanded. "He came up here to find dinosaurs. If there are any dinosaurs around here, they would appear to be in that enclosure. That's where we should look for him." She shivered slightly. "And I, for one, want to find him and get back to civilization."

"I think we can all agree on that," I said.

"Then what should we do?" Mr. Cartwright asked. "Walk up and knock on the gate?"

"I believe I have already said that I doubt the inhabitants of that place, if there are any, would welcome visitors." I thought for a moment, then said, "I think we should go around the enclosure. We should get a look at it from all sides, see what we can learn. How big is it? Are there other entrances? Who is in there? Is Mr. Hancock anywhere to be seen? Are there really dinosaurs inside it?"

Betsy nodded approval. Mr. Cartwright seemed less enthusiastic, but shrugged his acceptance. Annoyed, I suggested, "Perhaps, Mr. Cartwright, you would prefer to wait here with the mules? We will, of necessity, do our best to be back before nightfall." I thought we might do better without him, and our mounts could well be more hindrance than help in this venture.

"You're planning to be at this all day?" He glanced at the sun, perhaps halfway up the eastern sky.

"We might be," I said. I saw no point in elaborating that we had no idea how big the enclosure was, or how rough the surrounding terrain might be, or whether we might need to dodge sentries.

He hesitated, looking around, then agreed. "I suppose I could use a rest," he said.

"Good," I said. "Make camp or not, as you please, but do try to stay out of sight. And watch the mules; I don't want them stolen."

He nodded. I turned and discovered that Betsy was already on her way into the trees along the canyon wall. I followed, trying my best to make it appear that I was in no great hurry to catch up; I relied upon my longer legs to make up the distance between us.

Cartwright was not yet out of sight behind us when I came abreast of her.

We did not bother to speak at first; our route was obvious, given our plan and our surroundings. We came to the stockade soon enough and turned to follow it away from the gate.

From our starting point it extended some eighty yards, by my best estimate, through the forest, until it came to the canyon wall, where it was anchored to the stone with iron straps held by what appeared to be railroad spikes. It did not extend up the steep slope – or rather, the cliff, for any lesser term would not do that rocky barrier justice.

Betsy and I stood for a moment, looking up. "Whoever built this didn't bother to make a complete enclosure," she said.

"Why should they, when Mother Nature has provided this wall for them?" I replied.

"Because cliffs can be scaled," she answered.

"So can wooden walls."

"But it worries me, Tom – if the stockade is intended to keep people *out*, then this set-up has an obvious flaw. Someone could wander across the ridge to the top of that cliff and look right down into the enclosure."

"But if it was built to keep something *in*," I said, seeing her point, "then this arrangement would make sense. So you think this is not so much a fortress as a corral? For dinosaurs, perhaps?"

"It might be."

"Shall we ascend, then, and see what we find?"

I expected her to ask how I intended to climb that cliff, but I had once again underestimated her. "We shall," she replied, hitching up her skirts to display a delightful pair of ankles.

Her skirts were, in fact, something of a nuisance; women's clothing, even the more practical styles of the far West, was not really intended for this sort of activity. I knew that Betsy possessed some very unorthodox garments of her own design that were made for an engineer's use and were less restricting; she had worn them when operating her father's airship through the skies of Mexico. However, to the best of my knowledge she had not brought them with her on this trip, but had left them back East, since I had told her I was not planning on any activities where they would be needed. Instead she was wearing fairly traditional feminine attire. Nonetheless, she made her way upward with surprising speed.

I had actually thought we might scout back along the cliff face for an easier route, but Betsy was obviously not inclined to waste time on an indirect approach; she was already scrambling up the scree at the foot of the cliff, heading for the seam where the stockade met the stone.

I quickly saw why; the wooden beams had not been fitted very exactly to the stone, and the small gaps this left provided occasional handholds and footholds. She clambered up this seam as if it were a ladder.

"Where did you learn to do that?" I called up to her, keeping my voice low.

"Climbing around my father's machinery," she replied.

"It's quite amazing," I replied, as much to myself as to her. And in fact, it *was* amazing.

Betsy's smaller fingers and toes fit into the seam's crevices better than my own, so she was able to make good time until she reached the top of the barrier, some thirty feet or more off the ground. There she paused, looking for a way to continue her climb up the face of the cliff, finally at something of a loss, as I had expected her to be from the start.

As a boy I had been trained in climbing, back in the Adirondacks, as part of my preparation for a career as an adventurer, where I did not suppose Betsy had much experience in such things, despite her talk of clambering around machinery. A rocky cliff is quite different from any man-made framework. I thought I might be able to assist her once the artificial aid of the stockade was gone, and indeed she seemed hesitant, studying the rocks above her.

But she also glanced over the top of the stockade, almost incidentally – her attention was clearly on getting to the top of the cliff, rather than seeing what lay inside the enclosure – and there she froze, transfixed by what she saw.

Chapter Nine

Around the Enclosure

I hurried up the cliff as best I could, eager to see what had caught her attention so completely, but my greater bulk and larger extremities had me at a significant disadvantage despite my training, and it took me what seemed like several minutes to come up behind her - though in truth, it was probably not that long.

I could not use the joints between the cliff and the stockade as easily as she had, and I could not use the last few at all because she was occupying them, but I was able to find handholds on the cliff face itself that allowed me to pass her and peer over her head into the enclosure.

When I did, at first I saw nothing but trees and did not understand why she had stopped to stare. But then I shifted my gaze just a little, so that I was looking through a gap in the branches, and I found myself just as fascinated as she was.

"Do you think it's dead?" she asked.

"I don't know," I replied. "It might just be asleep."

What we were seeing, some distance away and mostly hidden

by the trees, was very large; we could not see its shape very clearly through the tangled branches of the pines, but we could tell we were looking at the shoulder and upper foreleg of some tremendous beast, one that stood at least ten or twelve feet high at that shoulder. Its hide was scaly and golden-brown in color and gleamed in the morning sun.

We could not see, from our perch, any of the head or neck; a stand of evergreens concealed them completely. Of the body beyond the shoulder we could catch only glimpses, flashes of golden-brown scales among the trees and brush.

It was not moving. I believe that was why Betsy had initially stared so intently – it was not mere surprise, but rather, she was watching for any sign of life. There was none; the thing was as still as the cliff above us.

"I don't see it breathing," Betsy said. "But we're probably too far away."

"If it's a dinosaur, then it's a sort of lizard, isn't it?" I asked.

"That's what the scientists say," Betsy replied.

"Lizards can be amazingly still. I've seen it, in zoos and menageries – they can be utterly motionless for several minutes, then move so quickly you can scarcely follow it. I read that it has something to do with being cold blooded."

"I wouldn't know," Betsy said. "When I went to the zoo as a little girl I spent my time watching the tigers and elephants, not visiting the reptile house, and there aren't many lizards living in the wild in New Jersey."

"There are a few," I responded. I had, as a boy, made a study of the wildlife in every part of the eastern United States. "In general, though, it's too cold."

"It's just as cold here in the Utah mountains, isn't it?"

I did not know the exact climatic differences between the two regions, but I certainly did not expect to see many lizards scuttling around the area. On the other hand, I knew rattlesnakes were native to the Utah Territory, and half a dozen other varieties of snakes as well, and there might well be lizards, too. "Perhaps dinosaurs don't mind the cold as much as their lesser cousins," I suggested.

"Or perhaps, appearances notwithstanding, that's not a dinosaur," Betsy retorted.

As it remained motionless, another possibility struck me. "You know, I'm not sure it's real," I said. "If it's dead, how is it still standing? If it's alive, how can even a reptile that size be so still, even asleep? I think it's a statue."

"What would a *statue* that size be doing out here?"

"What is this entire *enclosure* doing out here?"

She had no good answer for that. Instead she turned her attention upward and said, "Maybe we can get a better look at it from up there."

"Maybe we can," I agreed. "Here, see there, to your right? I think that's your next handhold."

With that we resumed our ascent, each providing the other with suggestions and guidance. Betsy's climbing ability astonished me, but I was not foolish enough to say so, and just a few minutes later we scrambled up onto a slope where, while we still dared not stand upright, we could proceed on hands and knees rather than clinging spider-like to the cliff face. Another twenty yards brought us to a surface that, while still not level, provided adequate footing. There we rose to our feet, and as one we turned to look back into the enclosure.

It was surprising how little we could see of its interior. Not only were there inconveniently placed trees, but the contour of the slope was such that most of the little canyon remained hidden below the curve of the land. What's more, there were swaths of drab, heavy fabric – probably tent canvas, but we could not tell for certain – stretched across a framework of some sort, hiding much of what lay below from our gaze. I could not judge with any certainty whether they were intended to provide shelter, or merely concealment.

"Well, there's more down there than just a stockade and a statue," Betsy remarked. "Come on."

I turned to follow as she headed along the ridge, and I noticed that the climb had left her clothing somewhat the worse for wear. I glanced down at my own attire and saw that it, too, had suffered; from chest to toe I was covered in dust, and the fabric of my garments was scraped and torn in dozens of places – mostly my coat, but the legs of my trousers had been damaged, as well. We had not taken the time to don protective gear before our climb, and this destruction was the result.

Such, I reminded myself, are the hazards of an adventurer's career.

We made our way largely along bare stone; the climb had apparently brought us above the local tree line, where the constant wind swept away soil and prevented any vegetation from taking root. I was uncomfortably aware that this left us visible to anyone for miles around who chanced to look in this direction.

I could not see anyone who might have spotted us, though. The surrounding peaks were barren and deserted. The canyon below us showed only pine trees, tangled shrubs, and canvas. I tried to locate that great brown beast we had glimpsed before, but could not discern it – the area where I estimated it to stand was completely hidden from this side by one of the largest expanses of yellowed cloth.

We proceeded along the stony promontory, walking at a steady pace, neither hurrying nor dawdling. With each step I peered down into the canyon, gazed quickly around at our immediate surroundings and the distant peaks to be sure we were not being watched, and then moved on and repeated this pattern.

We had gone perhaps a quarter of a mile when I called, "Wait." Betsy paused and looked back at me.

I pointed. "We might be able to climb down there."

She followed my gaze and saw what I had spotted – an area where the cliff had partially collapsed, providing an easier path down into the canyon. She nodded.

Moving cautiously, we made our way down the slope. At one point I slipped on loose rock and sent a shower of pebbles rattling down the cliff; we both froze, worried lest the sound alert guards below, but after a moment, when we neither saw nor heard any movement, we continued our descent.

I found myself regretting that we had left our ropes back with the mules, but it was not worth going back for them.

We were perhaps halfway down when we saw the barrier. This was no grand wooden stockade, but a network of sharpened timbers and barbed wire. We looked at one another.

"To keep out bears, do you suppose?" I asked quietly.

"To keep out *us*, more likely," Betsy replied.

"I think it was actually intended for *me*," a third voice said, in a louder, more conversational tone.

Startled, we both spun to find the source of this new sound and saw a ragged figure crouched in a nearby thicket, pointing a rifle at us. He wore a filthy, matted sheepskin vest and a battered, misshapen bowler hat. His features were largely obscured by a massive black beard as he squinted down the barrel of his weapon at us.

Then those eyes suddenly widened, and the rifle lowered an inch or two. "Tom Derringer?" he exclaimed. "And Miss Vanderhart?"

Despite the beard and his sorry condition, I finally recognized his voice. "Mr. Hancock?" I replied.

Although he was far thinner than when I had met him on the train half a year before, it was unmistakably Teddy Hancock. He must have lost a good twenty pounds; all his clothing, not merely the vest, was patched and filthy, and his bowler, already past its prime when I first met him, was no longer fit to be seen in public. There was a split in the toe of his left boot that revealed a grubby bit of woolen hose. His beard was a bristly mess, clearly not trimmed in months, and his greasy, unkempt hair was past his shoulders. A knapsack was slung on his back, and that, too, was somewhat the worse for wear.

I cannot adequately describe just how pleased, surprised, and relieved I was to see him; it seemed our quest had not been in vain, and that he had indeed survived the hazards of a winter alone in the mountains. My fears of wandering in the wilderness indefinitely and returning empty handed, or stumbling across a skeleton that might or might not be his, were put instantly to rest. We would be able to bring him back to Ogden in triumph, and I could collect my fee – the first money I had earned from my adventuring! It would hardly cover all the expenses I had incurred in my career to date, but it was a start. I'm fairly certain my face was covered with an absolutely ridiculous smile at the realization, though of course I couldn't see it.

Steady Teddy grinned in return, the barrel of the rifle drooping to point at the ground. But then his smile gave way to an expression of pure bafflement. "What are *you* doing here?" he exclaimed.

"Looking for you!" I replied.

"But I thought you were bound for California!"

"I was, and that's where your employers hired me to find you. Messrs. Murray, Holtzmann, and Clement were concerned about your extended absence."

"And they sent *you*? I'm delighted to see you, Mr. Derringer, but I hadn't thought you had any connection with those people."

"I'm afraid their usual man, John Beckwith, met with an unfortunate end a few months ago."

"I don't know any Beckwith." His grip on the rifle tightened slightly.

"He generally went by the name Justus Smith when dealing with your employers."

"Justus Smith?" That seemed to shake him. "I never met him, but I surely *heard* about him. You say Smith's dead? An unfortunate end, you called it. You killed him?"

"No, I did *not*," I retorted. "I'm no murderer, and though I confess we were at odds on occasion, to the point of aiming guns at one another, in the end he proved reasonable enough and gave me no cause to kill him. He was captured by a tribe of savages, however, and died trying to escape." I admit to some mild regret at referring to the Skyless and their multi-millennial civilization as "savages," but I could think of no better term just then.

"And you aren't in league with...these people?" He jerked his head in the direction of the enclosure's interior.

"Of course not! We don't even know who they are. That's one of the things we hope you can tell us."

He continued to hesitate, and there was a brief pause as we all considered our situation, and then Betsy added, "Our employers' friend and partner, Mr. Cartwright, chose to accompany us. He's watching the mules not far outside the big gate." She gestured toward the stockade at the canyon's mouth.

His face lit up with delighted amazement. "Cartwright? *Pete* Cartwright? He's here with you?"

I nodded.

I thought I saw Hancock's eyes moisten at that. "Show me," he said.

"Gladly," I said. "And then you must tell us all what you have done and seen all these months."

"Of course," he said.

Betsy leaned over and whispered, "Perhaps we should hear his story here and now, before we accompany him anywhere."

I shook my head and gestured toward the timbers and barbed wire. "There might be unwelcome eyes watching us." I waved toward the top of the slope. "Let's go."

We reversed our course and climbed back up, Teddy Hancock moving in parallel a few yards away. At the top he waited for us to join him, and the three of us marched side by side toward the wall, all of us keeping a wary eye on our surroundings.

Our descent was a little less organized. When Betsy and I

began to lower ourselves down toward the barrier, Mr. Hancock balked. "*Here?*" he exclaimed.

"Come on," Betsy called.

Mr. Hancock grimaced. "I'm willing to give it a try, Miss, but it wouldn't have been my first choice."

"Oh, it's fine," she insisted.

Reluctantly, he slung his rifle on his shoulder and followed, but his climbing skills, rather to my surprise, were not up to the task, and he slipped, sending a scattering of pebbles down the cliff before he was able to catch himself on an outcropping. He let out a nervous chuckle, then gathered his wits, and as I waited nearby he resumed his descent.

Betsy had not waited; she was clambering down the corner between the cliff and the stockade like a squirrel down a tree. Hancock and I followed more slowly and carefully. We were near the bottom when he lost his footing one final time and tumbled to the ground before the barrier.

I was concerned that he might have injured himself, or that the sound might bring unwanted attention, but he sprang to his feet, brushing dust from his vest as he looked around. Betsy stood nearby, and they both waited, alert to their surroundings, as I completed my descent and joined them.

A moment later we were moving again, and not long after we came in sight of Mr. Cartwright and our mules.

Mr. Cartwright had been leaning comfortably against a tree, but at the sight of us he jerked upright. He stared, eyes wide, at our new companion.

And Mr. Hancock, for his part, stopped and stared, as well.

"Pete?" he said. "They told me you had come, but...you're no adventurer! What are *you* doing here?"

"Looking for *you*, you fool," Mr. Cartwright replied. Then he stepped forward and clasped Hancock in a hearty embrace, ignoring his dishevelment. "And I am *so* glad we've found you!"

When that display of emotion finally ended and the two men

released their hold, Hancock said, his voice cracking, "You came after *me*? Why?"

"We were worried about you! The committee doesn't like it when our friends vanish without explanation. We thought you'd be back by Christmas!"

"Well, I wasn't inclined to come back empty-handed when I'd actually *seen* the blasted creatures!" He waved toward the stockade.

Betsy and I exchanged glances. "I don't understand," I said. "If you found the dinosaurs, then what else did you want out here?"

Mr. Hancock's mouth twisted wryly. "Well, among other things, I didn't have any *proof*, Mr. Derringer," he replied. "I had lost my camera in a storm early on, you see, so I wanted some other solid evidence and just couldn't seem to get my hands on any. I could never get close enough to get a really good look, and I never found so much as a shed scale as hard evidence. I have never yet figured out where those things do their business when nature calls, so I didn't even have *that*. Not to mention, by the time I was sure I wasn't imagining them I had no idea where I was, and I was afraid that if I went back to Ogden I'd never find my way back here again. Once winter closed in I was too busy just staying alive to do much of anything else, particularly when I didn't dare leave any footprints in the snow."

"Why didn't you want to leave footprints?" Betsy asked. "Did you think the dinosaurs might track you down and eat you?"

Hancock shook his head. "No, not the dinosaurs. I haven't seen any meat eaters, just a couple of Stegosaurus and the big one that I think was a Brontosaurus – all herbivores. Or it might have been an Apatosaurus, or something else in that family, but definitely a plant eater. Yes, I studied up on them before I came out here, so I know what they are." He smiled. "They look just like the pictures."

That startled me, given that every picture in existence was

merely an artist's interpretation of scientific guesswork, and I would not expect great accuracy from such depictions. But I did not say anything. Perhaps the artists and scientists had somehow gotten them exactly right, for once.

"It wasn't the dinosaurs that concerned me," Hancock concluded.

"What, then?" Betsy demanded.

"The Danites," he said.

Chapter Ten

Mr. Hancock's Tale

At those words Mr. Cartwright stepped back, an expression of shock on his face. "Teddy, there aren't any more Danites. There haven't been for more than forty years."

I had heard the name, but knew very little about the Danites. I knew they were one of the more violent and secretive organizations within the Church of Jesus Christ of Latter-Day Saints in its early years, well before the migration west and the founding of Salt Lake City, but that was almost all I could recall. They had been intended to defend the church against its oppressors, I remembered that much, and I was busily trying to dredge up anything more that I might have heard about them when Betsy asked, "What are the Danites? Some local tribe?"

"They're the Mormon vigilante militia," Mr. Hancock replied.

"And they were disbanded in 1838, before my people even left Missouri!" Mr. Cartwright protested.

"There have been rumors to the contrary," I said hesitantly.

In fact, I did not know the truth of the matter, and I am not sure anyone did, but there had indeed been reports off and on that the Danites had continued to exist long after the band's supposed dissolution, and that they were responsible for various acts of violence, including multiple murders. Some claimed they had had a hand in the infamous Mountain Meadow Massacre of 1857, though that was generally attributed entirely to a different group called the Nauvoo Legion.

Mr. Cartwright turned on me in a startling display of wrath, a great contrast to the warm affection he had just displayed to Mr. Hancock, or to the calm, if somewhat unhappy, demeanor we had lived with the past few days. "There are *always* rumors!" he exclaimed. "No matter what we do, there are lies and stories and slander! We are accused of every sort of inhumanity and horror, when all we want to do is live in peace by the tenets of our faith! Do you know that even now, our president is being persecuted by the federal government, forced to live apart from his family, for following our customs?"

"What?" Betsy asked, obviously baffled. "What are you talking about?"

"Plural marriage, I suppose," I said. "Congress outlawed it a year or so back."

"It's been over two years now, Mr. Derringer," Mr. Hancock said apologetically. I realized he was probably right; spending months in captivity had thrown off my reckoning of time.

"The Edmunds Act," Mr. Cartwright said, in a tone of absolute disgust. "They made polygamy a felony. And John Taylor, the leader of our faith, has left his wives and children to comply with this law. Though even that may not be enough for the hypocrites in Washington."

"What does that have to do with these Danites?" Betsy asked.

"Nothing!" Mr. Cartwright said, throwing up his hands. "There aren't any Danites! It's just another slander against our faith."

"Rumor has it," Mr. Hancock said, with an uneasy glance at his friend, "that there are armed bands of Mormons hiding in these mountains, ready to put up a fight if the government in Washington sends federal troops in to enforce the Edmunds Act.

Some people call these bands Danites. There are other names, as well – Avenging Angels, Destroying Angels, Vigilance Committees, and so on – but back East I mostly heard them called Danites."

"They don't exist," Mr. Cartwright said flatly.

Hancock cocked his head to one side and eyed his friend. "I don't like to argue, Pete, but then who do you think built that stockade around the bend over there?" he said, gesturing in the direction we had just come from. "Who is it that I've seen and heard and hidden from all winter, coming and going out here in the wilderness?"

Mr. Cartwright opened his mouth and started to speak, then stopped. He could not very well deny the evidence of his own eyes; that stockade was clearly real. He hesitated, then asked, "Why do you think those people are Saints?"

"Well, to begin with, Pete, we're in the Utah Territory," Mr. Hancock replied.

He was clearly about to say more, but I interrupted. "We might have crossed into Wyoming," I ventured.

He waved the notion aside. "Even so, it's Mormon country. Who else could they be?"

"One of the local tribes, maybe?" Mr. Cartwright suggested. "Or some gang of outlaws, sheltering here?"

"They looked pretty white to me," Mr. Hancock said. "And they've been bringing up supplies and men from that direction." He pointed. "Which you surely know as well as I do is where Ogden and Salt Lake City lie, and just about everyone there is Mormon. Or Saints, if you prefer."

"It may be, Mr. Cartwright," I suggested, "that there are secrets within your church to which you are not privy."

At that, Mr. Cartwright seemed to deflate, slumping forward. "I...suppose there might be," he conceded. "But I won't believe in Danites until I see them with my own eyes and hear them claim that name."

"Well, that's fine, Pete," Mr. Hancock said. "If that name

troubles you so much, I don't reckon we need to use it, but call them what you will, they are armed men, men who built that stockade, and who have been living in there as long as I've been in the area. That's who I was avoiding all winter."

Betsy had been listening to all this and had clearly been thinking about what she heard. Now she spoke up.

"Tom," she said, "the tracks we followed led into that stockade."

"Yes," I agreed.

"Teddy says he's seen dinosaurs, so we can assume that's what made the tracks. And we both saw *something* in there, a huge creature of some sort, even if we can't be sure it was a dinosaur."

"We did."

"And Teddy says that these Danites, or whoever they are, are living in there."

"Yes," I repeated.

"Then have they somehow captured a dinosaur?"

I turned to Teddy Hancock. "*Have* they?"

"That's what I wanted to *tell* you, Mr. Derringer, before we went off the track with all that talk about whether these are Danites or some other militia."

"Then tell us," I said.

"Well, they haven't just captured *one* dinosaur," he answered. "They've captured *all* of them – or at any rate, I haven't seen the slightest sign of any dinosaur that *isn't* kept penned up in that stockade. *That's* the main reason I stayed out here and didn't go back to Ogden to put together a hunting party – quite aside from finding the place again, I wouldn't know who I could trust and who I couldn't, as any Mormon I could meet might be a part of whatever group it is that built that fort. And they haven't just *captured* them, Mr. Derringer; they've *tamed* them. When the dinosaurs come out for their exercise, or whatever it is they do, they have guards, but they aren't bound with ropes or chains or any sort of harness; they just go where they please, and then *go back to the stockade*, unprompted, without anyone forcing them or even leading them. It's as if they're *pets*. Pets the size of a house."

I simply stared at him for a moment, unable to come up with any sensible reply to such a fantastic claim.

"Or perhaps," Betsy ventured, after a brief silence, "it is these men who are pets, and the dinosaurs are in charge."

Mr. Cartwright turned to her with an expression of astonishment. "Are you suggesting dinosaurs might be *intelligent*?"

"Why not?" Betsy replied, her expression defiant.

"Do their skulls not show them to have possessed very small brains?" I asked.

She hesitated, then admitted, "Yes. They do." She paused no more than a second or two before saying, "but how do we know that their brains operated in the same fashion as our own? Perhaps they had additional brain material somewhere other than inside their skulls."

"I think it far more likely that it is the humans who have tamed the beasts," I said.

"Fine," Betsy said. "But I think we really must keep in mind that we know almost nothing about these creatures and should not be careless in our assumptions."

"Fair enough," I replied.

"If you two are done with your nonsense..." Mr. Hancock said.

"Yes?" I asked.

"Whoever is in charge, the dinosaurs and the Dan...these people are working together, and ever since the snow began to melt I've been trying to get a look inside that compound of theirs to see what the devil they're up to in there."

"That's why you're still out here?" Mr. Cartwright asked.

"Yes."

"To be honest," I said, "I don't particularly *care* why you're out here. I was hired to bring you safely back to Ogden, and that's what I intend to do. Let someone else deal with these mysterious men and monsters."

"What?"   Mr. Hancock turned to stare at me in open-mouthed astonishment. "I'm not going anywhere until I find out what those people are up to!"

"I don't want to resort to force, Mr. Hancock," I said gently.

His expression turned grim, and his rifle slid from his shoulder. He reached across to catch it. "What makes you think you can force me, Mr. Derringer?" he asked, his hands closing on the weapon.

"There are three of us, and only one of you," I began.

"Wait, Mr. Derringer," Mr. Cartwright said, before I could continue.

I turned to look at him.

"Given that I don't reckon we can capture them and make a fortune, since it looks as if they have already been captured, I am not tremendously interested in the dinosaurs," Cartwright said, "or whatever those things are, but these men and their stockade – what are *they* doing here? How did they tame these creatures? Are they indeed Mormons, as you call us, or on the other hand, could they perhaps be some threat to the Saints? I agree with Teddy; we should learn a little more about them before we go back."

I confess that I felt a twinge of annoyance. The question of just who or what was in that stockade, and why, was admittedly an interesting one, but it was not what we had come for nor what we were equipped for. "That was no part of my agreement with your compatriots," I protested.

"The circumstances have changed," he replied. "If it's about your fee, I will pay you an additional hundred dollars to find out who these people are and what they want."

I had been thinking, insofar as I had considered the matter at all, that once I had delivered Mr. Hancock safely back to Ogden and collected my pay I might see about suggesting another expedition to investigate this place, but I had not decided on whether I wanted to participate in it myself, and I had certainly not intended to attempt such an investigation without further preparation. Still, we were *here*, even if there were only the four of us, and even if we had equipped ourselves for a search and a rescue, not an infiltration. I glanced at Betsy, who shrugged. "I'm curious too, Tom," she said.

I sighed. "I suppose we could take a look," I said.

Chapter Eleven

Behind the Barrier

We decided that we had been standing on or near that open path quite long enough and took shelter among the trees, away from the track and well out of sight. We did not unburden the mules; we were well aware that a quick departure might become advisable.

"Didn't you have a mount of your own?" Betsy asked Mr. Hancock as we tethered our beasts of burden to a handy tree.

He nodded. "A horse," he said. "A mare."

"Is she at your campsite?"

"No." He clearly did not wish to elaborate.

Betsy, however, was not ready to let the matter rest. "Then..." she began.

"I told you I didn't dare leave tracks in the snow," Mr. Hancock interrupted, not meeting her gaze. "So I couldn't very well go hunting, could I?"

Betsy's hand flew to her mouth in perhaps the most feminine gesture I had ever seen her make. "Oh," she said.

"You ate your horse?" Mr. Cartwright asked, looking shocked.

"Yes, I ate her," Mr. Hancock said, carefully not looking at Betsy. "Didn't have any way to feed her, anyhow."

"One less complication to worry about," I remarked.

Betsy threw me a disgusted look, but said nothing. Messrs.

Hancock and Cartwright both seemed surprised that she said no more about the horse, but I knew better. Despite her initial startlement she was a realist, more so than any of we mere men, and she understood the exigencies Mr. Hancock must have faced.

With that discussion concluded, and the mules secured, the four of us settled to the ground in a cluster of pines, reasonably well hidden from anyone who might pass by.

"Well, Mr. Hancock," I said, once we were all fairly comfortable, "you know more about the situation here than the rest of us. What would you suggest for our next step?"

"I can't say I have any brilliant ideas, Mr. Derringer," Hancock admitted. "I've been out here for weeks, trying to catch one of the men alone, or to get a close look at the dinosaurs without being spotted, but I haven't managed it. They've been very careful, always traveling in groups – that is, the men travel in groups of three or more, and while the dinosaurs usually emerge one at a time, they are always accompanied by two or three men. I've tried to find a way into the compound, but I haven't managed that, either. I thought about cutting or digging my way through the barbed wire, but they do have guards patrolling the perimeter; every time I thought I might have found a spot where I could get in unnoticed, a sentry would walk past and look straight at it. I supposed I might be able to get in *between* patrols, but I hadn't worked out a time and place I felt sure of, and I haven't cared to risk it. I've been searching for hidden entrances with no luck. Maybe you can give us a new perspective and suggest something I've missed."

I considered for a moment, then said, "Perhaps we could simply talk to them, and ask them why they're here."

"Mr. Derringer, now that I've had some time to consider, I think it's pretty clear that they're *hiding* out here," Mr. Cartwright said. "I don't think they'll take kindly to such an inquiry."

"But are they hiding from *us*? If they really are polygamous Mormons, well, we aren't federal troops. We mean them no harm."

"But they don't - " Mr. Cartwright began.

"John Thomas Derringer," Betsy interrupted, "how stupid *are* you?"

"What?" I said, startled.

"Haven't you learned *anything* on your adventures? Has the honest and direct approach of which you are so idiotically fond *ever* worked out well?"

"I don't -" I began, but she was having none of it. She had not finished speaking and was not going to let me talk until she had said her piece.

"You got my father's flying machine shot out of the sky with your honesty. We wound up as captives of the Maya, and then captives of Hezekiah McKee, and we just spent *months* as prisoners of the Skyless, because you don't have the sense to stay out of sight and keep your mouth shut. I am *not* going along while you march up to a bunch of armed strangers and politely ask what they're doing, hiding out here in the wilderness!"

"I wasn't going to!" I managed to say, before she continued.

"Besides, haven't you been listening to what Teddy's been telling us? He said there are *men* in that stockade - if they're polygamists, where are the *women*? The children?" She turned to Hancock. "Mr. Hancock, have you seen or heard any women or children?"

"No, I..." He glanced at me. "I haven't. But they might be locked away in there."

"Betsy," I said, "*I* wasn't going to talk to them. But I thought that Mr. Cartwright might approach them as a fellow Mormon, while the rest of us stood watch from a safe distance with our guns, ready to open fire if they prove hostile."

Betsy glared at me, then relaxed slightly. "Well," she acknowledged, "that's not *as* stupid. But I still think it's a bad idea."

"*I'm* certainly not very enthusiastic about it, either," Mr.

Cartwright said. "What if they aren't Saints at all? What if they decide to just shoot me?"

"I don't think we'd want to take on the whole lot of them," Mr. Hancock said. "I've kept track of how many different men I've seen come and go, and I make it at least twenty."

I frowned. "That's more than I would have guessed," I admitted. "I'd agree that we don't want to simply walk up and knock on their gate. But you said that you've seen them outside the stockade?"

Mr. Hancock nodded.

"Perhaps Mr. Cartwright could talk to one of those groups, out of sight of their fortress – just a traveler making conversation."

The others exchanged glances. Eventually Betsy broke the silence. "It's not *completely* idiotic," she acknowledged. "But there's no reason to think they would tell a stranger the truth about whatever it is they're doing out here."

"She's right," Mr. Hancock said. "They probably have some story prepared."

I could see that he was almost certainly correct in that. I sighed and thought some more, and something occurred to me.

"Mr. Hancock," I said, "how big is that enclosure?"

"What? Oh, not so very large, really. Once you're past the walls and barbed wire it's maybe three or four acres inside the canvas."

"And you said you'd seen at least two Stegosauruses and one Brontosaurus?"

"That's right. Or at least I think it's a Brontosaurus."

"Those are very large animals, are they not?"

"Size of a house, Mr. Derringer. The Brontosaurus is the size of a confounded mansion."

"And they stay inside the stockade most of the time?"

"Almost *all* the time, really. I've never seen more than one outside at a time, and I've only seen *any* of them come out maybe once or twice a week. Could've missed a few, I suppose."

I nodded. "That was the impression I had from what you had said before. Which leaves me with a question: What do they *eat*?"

Hancock stared at me for a moment, then said, "I've never seen them eat."

"When they have come out, they have not been grazing?"

He shook his head. "Not a nibble," he said. "Never seen one open its mouth – which I had wanted to, to get a look at their teeth, so I'm sure of it."

"Does that seem *possible*? What are they feeding them in there? Could four acres support three of these gigantic beasts?"

"Could they be hibernating?" Betsy asked. "The one we glimpsed from the cliff wasn't moving."

"If they're hibernating, then why have I seen them at all?" Hancock said.

"Could the men be bringing in fodder?" Mr. Cartwright suggested.

"I haven't seen any," Mr. Hancock said. "Going by the markings on the barrels, the supply wagons I've seen mostly seem to have salt beef, flour, and coal."

"Well, couldn't they eat flour?" Betsy asked.

"Or the barrels might be deliberately mislabeled," Mr. Cartwright said.

"We came here following tracks, but we found those tracks because we heard a sound," I said. "A hiss. Was that the dinosaurs?"

Hancock shrugged. "Most likely it was. I've heard them hiss, both inside the walls and when they're out walking. It's loud, and harsh, and it's not like any animal I ever heard. Sounds almost like a steam train."

"Do they make any other cry? A roar, perhaps?"

He shook his head. "No. Just a hiss every once in awhile."

That sound – "almost like a steam train" – and other details were starting to come together. The beginnings of a theory were beginning to stir in the back of my mind. Barrels of coal – why would they haul coal out here, instead of cutting firewood close at hand? I remembered what I had seen earlier that morning, both on the trail and over the top of the stockade. I realized what I had found odd about the prints we had followed. "Have you ever taken a good look at their tracks?" I asked.

Mr. Cartwright said, "What are you after, Mr. Derringer? I thought we were concerned with the *men*, not their monstrous livestock."

"I don't think we can separate the two, Mr. Cartwright. Mr. Hancock, have you studied their tracks?"

"I wouldn't say *studied*, Mr. Derringer, but I've taken a look at them."

"Did anything about them strike you as *peculiar*?"

He looked at me with an expression of bafflement. "They were *dinosaur tracks*, Mr. Derringer. How could they be anything *but* peculiar?"

"When you saw the dinosaurs, how good a look at them did you get?"

"Not as good as I might have liked, I'll admit. Each beast was accompanied by two or more alert riflemen, so I could not get very close at all, and it was always after dark. Usually clouded over, as well."

"How did they move? Were they quick, like a lizard?"

"Great heavy things like that? Of course not. They were huge plodding creatures, with a slow, clumsy motion."

"Have you ever seen anything else move like that? Is there a comparison you can make to help me picture it?"

He thought for a moment, then shook his head. "Can't think of one. Sorry."

My theory was coalescing, but I did not think it was time yet to share it – but then Betsy said, "Oh!"

"What?" I asked, startled.

"I think I...well, I haven't seen them, except that one glimpse, so I can't be sure, but those tracks..."

"What about the tracks?" Mr. Hancock asked.

"They're too smooth," she said.

That was exactly what I had noticed myself, and had combined that observation with the sight of that motionless shoulder, and with the labels on the barrels, and with Mr. Hancock's description.

Mr. Cartwright said, "What?"

"I'm no tracker," she replied, "but I've seen animal tracks, and they're shaped by the bottom of the animal's foot."

"Yes, of course," Mr. Hancock said.

"But those footprints were *flat*. The bottom was absolutely smooth. What sort of animal has completely flat feet, with no pads or toes or joints of any kind?"

"There were toes," Cartwright objected.

I shook my head. The front of each print had three pointed projections obviously meant to represent toes, but even *these* had been smooth on the bottom and not properly separated from the rest of the track.

"It's artificial," I agreed. "No natural animal has feet that flat."

"What do you mean?" Mr. Cartwright demanded. "Do you think it was wearing *shoes?*"

"That's one possibility," I said, getting to my feet again. "I think it among the least likely, though."

"And what's *more* likely?"

"That these aren't real animals at all," I replied. "They're a fraud of some kind. Something intended to convince us that we are dealing with dinosaurs when we are not."

"That's *far* more believable than the idea that there are real living dinosaurs out here," Betsy said.

"Why would anyone..." Mr. Cartwright began, but then he stopped without completing the thought.

"I can think of three reasons," I said.

"To frighten people away," Betsy said.

"I'll admit I was pretty scared last night," Mr. Cartwright replied.

"That's one," I said. "Or they might be meant to lure people in."

"Well, how does *that* work?" Mr. Hancock asked, with a laugh. "Seems to me you can't have it both ways, Mr. Derringer. If it's scaring people away, it can't very well be luring them in."

"Can't it? *We're* here, aren't we?"

"Oh, but..." Mr. Hancock stopped, confused.

"It's unlikely they intended to do both," Betsy said. "If they meant to chase people away, I'd say they miscalculated."

"But it's the sort of miscalculation people can make," I said.

Betsy nodded, and said, "That's two. What's your third reason?"

"To sell something," I said. "Some people will do pretty much anything if they think there's money in it."

"That overlaps with the others, doesn't it?" Betsy asked.

"It does," I admitted. "Someone might mean to sell a foolproof defense against dinosaurs, or sell chances to see these fraudulent creatures."

"Or sell dinosaur tonic," Betsy suggested. "Animals that have survived fifty million years, why, their blood must just be *full* of good medicine!"

"I hadn't even thought of that one," I acknowledged, "but you're right, that could be it."

"For any of those to work, people would need to know these things were out here," Mr. Cartwright protested. "But all we've had until now are a few vague reports, even before my partners and I started hushing them up. No one's been chased away, no one's been given a good look, and no one's been advertising their wares."

"Maybe they're not ready yet," I said. "After all, we've spotted these tracks as counterfeits pretty quickly."

"You're as certain as that they're counterfeits?" Mr. Hancock asked.

"Oh, yes. With those flat bottoms? They must be. You didn't see that?"

"I never got a good look at the tracks. I didn't dare get too close. There were always guards." He shifted uncomfortably. "And I'd seen them walking!" he said. "I didn't see any need to look at the tracks. They were walking! One was out just last night!"

"We heard it," I agreed. "We followed its tracks. And speaking of tracks, there's something else we didn't see along the trail we followed. You said they're plant eaters, didn't you?"

"That's what the scientists back at Yale say."

"Did you ever see any scat? Predators hide theirs, but plant eaters don't."

Mr. Hancock looked baffled. "Not a bit," he admitted. "But if they aren't animals, what *are* they? What sort of counterfeits are we talking about? *I've seen them walking!*"

"Machines," I said. "I think they're machines. You said yourself that their hisses are like the sounds steam engines make."

"*Machines?*"

"That's my hypothesis, yes."

Mr. Hancock, thunderstruck, began, "But they walk! They move their heads, and...but..." His voice trailed off, and he looked thoughtful, clearly trying to use his memories of what he had seen to resolve the question. I waited, as Betsy and Mr. Cartwright looked on.

"They do move a mite stiffly," Mr. Hancock admitted at last.

"Like machines," I said.

"If that's true, why do you suppose they had one of them out last night?" Betsy asked.

"You don't think they were trying to scare us?" Mr. Cartwright asked.

"I don't think they were trying to scare *anyone*," I replied. "I don't think they wanted to be seen or heard at all, or they wouldn't have come out in the middle of the night, in the rain, in pitch darkness."

"A test run, maybe?" Betsy suggested. "Just being sure everything worked?"

"That's as good a guess as any," I said. "If you let machinery sit unused for too long, it breaks down from rust and neglect."

"*That's* certainly true," Betsy acknowledged, and I was glad to have someone with her expertise confirming my belief.

"That's one thing every adventurer knows," I said. "All those stories about thousand-year-old traps that still work as if they were new - they're mostly nonsense, intended to make us sound more daring than we really are. Most old traps don't work anymore."

Mr. Hancock nodded. "True enough," he said. "I've found old traps in temples that were jammed up with sand, or the ropes had rotted out and counterweights fallen away, or a hundred other things had gone wrong. Oh, some are still dangerous, but there's usually more risk from things that hadn't been *intended* as traps in the first place, since *those* break down, too." He hesitated. "You really think they're machines? You haven't even seen them!"

"*You* have," Betsy said. "What do *you* think?"

"I thought...I thought that was just how dinosaurs moved. After all, who would know?" He slumped. "But...perhaps they *could* be."

"Really?" Mr. Cartwright asked.

Mr. Hancock nodded. "*Amazing* machines, like nothing I'd ever seen before, better than the best side-show automaton I ever saw, but...yes, they could be machines."

"Well, then," Mr. Cartwright said cheerfully. "There aren't any dinosaurs here after all!"

"But there's still that mysterious stockade," Betsy reminded him.

"That's true," Mr. Cartwright acknowledged, "and I know I said we should investigate it, but on reflection, I'm not sure how we could go about that. If there aren't any dinosaurs - well, we can all go home and sleep in decent beds and worry about the enclosure later. We might ask around in some of the mountain towns and see if anyone knows anything."

While I had thought myself that going back to Ogden to regroup and resupply was wise, I was startled to hear Mr. Cartwright take a position so different from just a few moments before. I thought that perhaps it was not so much that he had reconsidered as that he had lost his nerve. Perhaps the idea of facing men who could build the sort of machines we were talking about was more daunting to him than the prospect of dinosaurs and ordinary frontiersmen.

Mr. Hancock blinked, then stared at Mr. Cartwright for a moment. He shook his head. "Oh, no, Pete," he said. "Whether they're living animals or machines, there's still something out here that looks like a pack of dinosaurs, and I want to know more about them. The people behind that stockade know what they are and why they're here, and I intend to get some answers. I'm not going back empty handed after all this."

"Oh, now, Teddy," Mr. Cartwright said. "What do you have in mind? We can't just walk in and demand explanations."

"I wasn't planning to walk in."

"Then what were you planning?" I asked.

"Well, I haven't thought it all out yet, but I have an idea."

"What sort of an idea?" Betsy asked.

"If you three are right, and those things are machines, then I don't just want explanations," Mr. Hancock said, his face determined. "I'm after something a little more tangible."

Betsy and I exchanged glances.

"What do you mean?" Mr. Cartwright asked uneasily.

"If those things are machines," Mr. Hancock said, "then I intend to take one back to Ogden with me."

Chapter Twelve

A Fresh Challenge

"*T*ake one?" I said. "Are you serious?"

"Maybe we should just go straight back to Ogden after all," Betsy said.

"Miss Vanderhart, I have been through a Hell of a winter up here," Mr. Hancock said. "I am not eager to let it all go for naught. If those dinosaurs are really machines that can walk and move about like animals – those could be worth a fortune!"

"To *whom*?" I asked, annoyed.

"P.T. Barnum, for one," Hancock retorted.

I could hardly gainsay *that*.

"If we can take possession of one of them and get it back to civilization, we can probably sell it for hundreds, maybe *thousands*."

"But it would be stealing!" Mr. Cartwright protested.

"It would be treasure hunting."

"That's stealing!"

"We don't know where those machines came from," he said. "I haven't seen any evidence of a metal foundry or fancy machine shop in that fort over there. You think a bunch of uneducated westerners could build things like that? They probably *found* them out here somewhere. They might be a relic of some lost civilization – don't your holy books talk about lost tribes coming to

America, Pete?"

"Well, after a fashion, but there's nothing in there about *dinosaurs*, either flesh or metal. The lost tribes didn't have anything like that."

"Then maybe it was some *other* lost tribe. Derringer, back me up on this – haven't there been lost civilizations in this country?"

"Of course there have," I said, throwing Betsy a glance. "Betsy and I have seen the proof. We haven't been there ourselves, but we've spoken to a man who visited El Dorado."

"But we never heard anything about mechanical dinosaurs," Betsy said. "And weren't you just saying that ancient mechanisms break down? If you're suggesting they were built by some long-lost pre-Columbian civilization, wouldn't they be so much scrap metal by now?"

"Maybe they were built by a completely *unknown* civilization," Mr. Hancock suggested, "one that had mechanical science we can scarcely imagine."

"But then why would they need to march them around the countryside, if not for maintenance?" I asked.

"Why would a lost tribe build mechanical dinosaurs in the first place?" Betsy asked.

"As draft animals, maybe," Mr. Hancock said.

"Why make them look like *dinosaurs*?" I asked.

"Because maybe there were *real* dinosaurs around that they modeled them on. Maybe they're that old."

"That brings us back to the question of maintenance," Betsy said.

"Then perhaps it wasn't an *ancient* civilization at all!" Mr. Hancock exclaimed, clearly struck by a new notion. "Aren't there stories of strange peoples living deep underground? In his story *Journey to the Center of the Earth*, that Frenchman Jules Verne described explorers finding prehistoric creatures in caverns miles down; how do we know that was mere fiction?" He was becoming visibly more enthusiastic with every word. "What if M'sieu Verne had spoken with adventurers who had actually *seen* such a place, and he presented their experiences as fiction to preserve their secrets? And now someone out here in the wilds of the Utah Territory has contacted these subterraneans and acquired dinosaurs from them. Perhaps they really *are* dinosaurs, and we haven't seen any evidence of their food because what's *really* inside that enclosure is the entrance to vast underground feeding grounds."

"But the tracks..." Betsy began.

Mr. Hancock interrupted her. "Or if they *are* machines, perhaps they were built by these subterraneans!"

"Teddy, I..." Cartwright began, but a look from his friend struck him dumb.

"We don't actually *know* whether they're machines, I agree," I said, "and we have even less reason to think that they were built by some lost civilization. This is all guesswork. It might be nothing but your overheated imagination."

"Then we should find out if it is!"

Again, I had no counter worth saying.

"How do you propose we do that?" Betsy demanded. "You've been out here alone for months and haven't managed a good look at them!"

"Ah, but Miss Vanderhart, I'm not *alone* anymore!"

"I don't think I like where this is going," Cartwright muttered.

"I never dared approach when one was out for its regular night-time march," Hancock continued, "because they always had two or three guards with them. Even with the element of surprise, I wasn't eager to take on two or more armed men – and of course, I didn't know what the dinosaur itself might do. But with three of us...or is it four?" He tipped his bowler. "Forgive me, Miss Vanderhart, but I don't..."

"Four," I said.

Betsy glared at me, clearly displeased that I had presumed to speak for her, but she did not contradict me.

"Well, then, the four of us, with surprise on our side, ought to be able to take on a couple of guards and a big clumsy machine."

"We don't know what these things are capable of!" Betsy protested. "How can you be sure they're clumsy?"

"I've *seen* them, Miss Vanderhart," Mr. Hancock said. "They're stiff and slow."

"Even if the machine itself isn't a threat," I said, "what about the men *inside* it? If it's a machine, someone must be inside the confounded thing, controlling it, and if they're as big as you say there could be three or four men in there!"

"More than that," Mr. Hancock admitted. "I hadn't thought of that. Though the machinery must take up most of the interior, so it couldn't be more than half a dozen in the Stegosaurus, maybe twice that in the Brontosaurus."

"And are these machines *armed?*" I asked. "They might be walking gunboats, with hidden ports concealing six-pounders or Gatling guns."

"I...don't think so," Mr. Hancock said. "Remember, I thought they were living animals. I didn't see anything that looked like a gunport, or any other sort of weapon, unless you count the spiked tail on the Stegosaurus."

"How good a look did you get?" Betsy asked.

Mr. Hancock frowned and did not answer.

"We could talk it over back in Ogden..." Mr. Cartwright began.

"No, Pete," Mr. Hancock said, cutting him off. "I am not going back to Ogden until I know whether those things are lizards or machines, and who's responsible for them. In everything I've seen them do, they've been slow and stiff. If we catch them by surprise we can capture a dinosaur's escort, and whoever's inside the machine – if it is a machine – won't dare harm us. We can ask a few questions, and then see what we learn."

"Wait," Betsy asked. "You want us to take the guards hostage?"

"Well...yes, Miss Vanderhart, I do, if only long enough for us to get a good look at one of their dinosaurs. I don't mean to hurt them, just hold them until we have answers."

"Well, it's not as stupid as letting *us* be taken prisoner," she acknowledged.

"I want to get a good, close look at one of those things," Hancock insisted. "Do you have a better suggestion for how I might do that?"

The three of us exchanged glances, but it was clear that none of us did, nor did we have any hope of dissuading Mr. Hancock. In fact, I think all of us shared a certain curiosity as to the nature and origin of these mysterious creatures. For myself, at least, I believed the rational thing to do would be to pack up and head for Ogden at once, with the intention of sending a larger and better equipped expedition later in the year, but I cannot honestly say that was what I *wanted* to do. I had promised Betsy that we were here merely to find Teddy Hancock and not to go adventuring after dinosaurs, but the mysteries surrounding their nature and origin had certainly provoked a good bit of wonderment, while the stockade that housed them, and the men that accompanied them, further aroused my natural inquisitiveness. I did not really think that Mr. Hancock's wilder speculations would prove to have any truth in them, but even the slightest possibility of finding an entrance to the wonders inside the earth, or the remnants of some long-lost but highly advanced civilization, tempted me to give his scheme a try.

As I considered this, another possibility occurred to me, inspired by my earlier adventures in Mexico and the Arizona Territory. Perhaps at one time the Lost City of the Mirage had manifested somewhere in these mountains, and *that* was the source of the dinosaurs, whether they were flesh or machinery. There were certainly still mysteries to be found in that peripatetic metropolis, though I had never heard of anyone seeing anything saurian there.

I debated whether to mention this new hypothesis to the others and decided against it, at least for the nonce. Mr. Hancock was quite enthusiastic enough about his own theories without adding mine to the mix.

And even before we had begun spinning these fantastic yarns of their origins, even before concluding that the dinosaurs were probably clever machines, we had agreed we should investigate further, even if that plan did not originally involve capturing anyone for questioning.

If it developed that these creatures, whether mechanical or flesh and blood, rightfully belonged to the inhabitants of that stockade, then we had no right to take them and would do our best to leave peacefully. If they had originated somewhere else or were even thinking beings in their own right, though, then it would not be theft at all to take one back to Ogden as a prize.

I thought I saw on Betsy's face that she was swayed by Mr. Hancock's plan. Had she been certain that a warm welcome awaited back at her family home in New Jersey I think she might have insisted on a more cautious path, but as it was...

And she loved machinery. When she thought the dinosaurs were beasts she had taken no great interest in them, but the possibility that they had been *engineered*, whether by modern Mormons or some people unknown to history – well, I believe she found that intriguing.

As for Mr. Cartwright, I'm not sure whether he approved, but he did not seem inclined to argue with Mr. Hancock any further.

But I did still have grave reservations on one point, though. "All right, we'll get a good look however we can, but we aren't going to take anything these people came by honestly. We aren't *thieves*, Mr. Hancock."

He smiled crookedly, his beard bristling even more than usual. "We aren't?"

"*I'm* not," I said.

"Well, what sort of an adventurer *are* you, then? Isn't half of what we do stealing treasure?"

"But that's...we don't take it from..."

I had started to say that while we did indeed rob tombs and ancient ruins we didn't steal from living people, but then I thought back on some of the accounts in my father's journals. He certainly stole from other thieves, and sometimes...

I had already noticed that adventurers did not always abide by civilized society's usual moral codes, nor were we expected to. Mr. Hancock's theory that mechanical dinosaurs must have been built by someone other their current owners, and that we would therefore only be stealing from thieves, was very tempting, and certainly had some basis in what we had observed. Still, I did not want to abandon all ethics completely.

Well, if the people behind the stockade were the rightful owners, we could stop short of carrying off their property, or perhaps we might pay them back somehow for anything we took. If this was the only way I could get Teddy Hancock back to Ogden without tying him onto a mule's back, then I'd do it – especially since I was as curious as anyone about just what these "dinosaurs" really were, where they came from, and why they were here.

"All right, then," I said. "Precisely what do you propose?"

In the end, the plan we settled upon was fairly simple. Since Mr. Hancock had spent so long observing the creatures, we relied on him to provide us with the basic information, and he was happy to oblige. Once every three or four days, he said – or rather, once every three or four *nights* – the gates in the stockade would open a few hours after sundown, and one of the monsters would march out, accompanied by two or three armed men who would walk alongside it. The thing would make its way a mile or two up the trail, moving at a pace its guards could match without undue effort, and then it would then turn around and return. Its speed might vary somewhat, and its precise movements were not always the same, but the fundamental routine did not change.

What we intended to do was to lie in wait at a point well away from the stockade, but one that every excursion reached before turning back or turning aside. We did not want to find ourselves waiting on one road while the monster took another, or watching as it turned back a hundred yards short of our position, but we wanted to be far enough from the enclosure that the escorts could not easily summon reinforcements. We studied the tracks along the trails as best we could, which was not very well, since the stony ground and recent rains had left little trace. This provided some information on the creature's past routes, and had the additional benefit of convincing Mr. Hancock that they were not, in fact, left by any normal animal. With that to guide us, in the end we settled on a piney thicket perhaps three-fourths of a mile from the gate as our ambuscade.

With the site chosen, we set up camp out of view of the trail and began our vigil. All four of us tried to get as much sleep during the day as we could, taking turns, so we would be alert when the moment came; then, at sunset, we took up our prearranged positions on either side of the trail and waited.

The first night ended in disappointment; we had nothing to show for our efforts but sore backs, tired eyes, and weary boredom from crouching silently in the dark. The second was no better, and the tedium became so great that more than one of us – I will not name names – broke with all protocol by quietly humming Stephen Foster tunes and familiar dance music. I kept myself amused by juggling small sticks; a good juggler, I knew, operates largely by feel, rather than by sight, so I thought it an appropriate pastime for those dark hours.

On the third night, however, we had been in position for perhaps three hours when I heard a loud but distant hiss.

"Hush!" I called, and we all froze, our senses alert.

For several minutes we saw and heard nothing more, but then came a slow, measured thudding, faint and far away but moving toward us in the dark. I crouched lower behind the shrub I had chosen for cover.

Another hiss sounded, louder and closer than before, as the thudding grew more audible. My muscles tensed. I risked a glance at Mr. Cartwright's post and could make out his dim outline. He was fumbling with a shuttered lantern. As the member of our party with the least experience with firearms, we had assigned him the duty of providing the light we would need for our ambush.

It had come as some surprise, and a little embarrassment on his part, to realize that Betsy did, in fact, have more experience with a gun than he did.

The thudding drew nearer, and now I could hear other sounds, as well – the crunch of booted footsteps, and a metallic ticking, as if some complex clockwork mechanism was approaching.

I could now see a faint glow some distance down the trail. Mr. Hancock had told us that when the moonlight was insufficient, as was the case tonight, one or more of the guards would carry a dim lantern. His best guess was that these used smoked glass to keep their radiance limited, and what I saw agreed with that description.

But I could also see a shape moving in the darkness near that faint light, a shape four or five feet off the ground that gleamed dully and moved in time to the thudding.

It was the size of a keg of nails lying on its side, but shaped like a lizard's head, the jaw bouncing slightly with every step, the glassy black eyes glittering in the dark, and behind it loomed a great dark mass.

I watched it approach, and the creature as a whole became more visible as it neared. That ticking and whirring, as if a clock was preparing to strike but never did, was oddly disturbing.

And then our quarry was in position. Teddy Hancock shouted, "Now!" and we rose up, weapons trained on the guards. Peter Cartwright clambered to his feet, still fumbling, and it was easily three or four seconds before he finally opened the shutter and shone the lantern upon the approaching monster.

"Drop your weapons!" I called, pointing my rifle at the nearest man. "We have you surrounded!"

Startled, the man did as he was told, raising his hands. One of those hands still held a smoked-glass lantern, so bringing his rifle to bear would have been difficult in any case, and he clearly had no interest in attempting it.

His companion on the creature's other side followed suit, as he found himself looking down the barrel of Mr. Hancock's gun.

A third man, who I had not previously noticed and who held no lantern, started to bring his own rifle up into position, only to find a pistol aimed at the side of his head from no more than a yard away.

"I wouldn't do that if I were you," Betsy said, and the third rifle fell to the ground as a third set of hands rose.

While this occurred the creature had taken another step or two, but now it stopped with a great hiss, venting smoke or steam from its nostrils. That was unmistakably the same hissing we had heard four nights previous. I tore my gaze from my disarmed opponent long enough to look at the monster.

It was, indeed, very much like the scientists' drawings of Stegosaurus, with crooked legs, a great humped body, and a double row of plates down its spine. While the head hung slightly below shoulder height, the center of its hump rose perhaps a dozen feet above the ground. The entire thing was covered in golden-brown scales that gleamed like polished brass in the lantern light, and it continued to tick and buzz as it stood there.

Those scales, I thought, might well *be* polished brass. Although it was remarkably lifelike in most regards, there could be no doubt that it was, in fact, a machine.

"Mr. C.," I said, preferring not to give our names as yet, "if you would be so kind as to collect the rifles these men dropped, and any other firearms you may find in their possession, I would esteem it a great favor."

"Yes, sir, Mr. De... Mr. D," Mr. Cartwright said. He stood the lantern on a convenient rock and set about his assigned task.

"Who are you people?" one of our captives asked, looking around. "I thought you were government troops, but they wouldn't send a woman!"

"Who are *you*?" I asked. "And what are you doing out here with this infernal machine?"

"We're..." he began.

One of his companions interrupted, "We are innocent men going about our own private business. What are you doing here?"

"We are investigating reports of dinosaurs," I said.

"And keeping an eye on you Danites," Mr. Hancock added, despite our agreement that I would be our spokesman.

"We aren't Danites!" one of them protested, but then he hesitated. "*Are* we?"

"We are not," the one who held no lantern said firmly. "The Danites were disbanded decades ago, before we were any of us even born. We are merely making peaceful preparations to defend our church, should it prove necessary."

"See?" Mr. Hancock exclaimed. "Danites!"

"Not everyone willing to fight for our faith is a Danite," Mr. Cartwright protested.

The ticking suddenly accelerated, and the Stegosaurus' immense head swung to one side. One of its front legs lifted and swung back, then landed with a thump.

"It's turning!" Betsy shouted.

"What's it doing?" Mr. Cartwright asked.

I found it oddly annoying, even in this tense moment, that Mr. Cartwright found it necessary to ask a question Betsy had already answered. I pointed my rifle at my captive's face, though I was careful not to put my finger on the trigger. "Tell your men inside that thing to stop, or we'll shoot."

"They can't hear us!" he protested.

"Mr. Derringer, that would be plain murder," Cartwright objected, ignoring our agreed upon rules about names. We stared as the mechanical dinosaur swung around, its long spiked tail slamming into a tree by the side of the trail. It curled the tail back, freeing it from the tree, and continued its turn.

"Mr. H.," I said, "I think we can handle the situation here, if you want to carry out your intention of getting a look inside that thing."

"How do I get inside it?" Mr. Hancock called. "I don't see a door!"

"Well, it wouldn't be a very convincing dinosaur if it had a great big obvious door in its side, would it?" Betsy shouted. "There's got to be a hatch *somewhere*, though - in the belly, maybe?"

"I don't see one," Mr. Hancock replied.

"Here, someone tie these three up," I said, as the Stegosaurus continued its rotation. I hurried to one side, looking for any sign of a seam or seal.

I tried to consider the situation logically. Big as it was, the creature's mouth and neck were clearly not broad enough to serve as an entrance to its interior for anyone, not even a child, and there were no other visible openings. I ducked down to look at its belly and had to agree with Mr. Hancock - there were no signs of a hatch to be found.

So the face provided no entrance, nor did the underside or either flank, and the tail narrowed far too much for a man to crawl through. That only left one possibility, and it was, in fact, the side that would be least visible. The entry had to be on top somewhere.

But how would one get to the top of the thing? Perhaps back in the enclosure they had a mounting platform of some sort, or even just a ladder that could be laid against its side, but out here there were no such conveniences. I thought about climbing a tree and dropping down on top of it...

And just then I had to duck, as it swung that spiked tail at me. While Mr. Cartwright might not be willing to kill these men without serious provocation, it appeared that someone inside that machine had no such reservations about killing us.

The tail passed harmlessly over my head, but then something whirred, and the spiked tip dropped three feet and came swinging back toward me.

This time, though, I had my own plan, and as the spikes approached my legs I leapt upward and flung myself forward, landing atop the swinging tail. I had to drop my rifle, but I managed to throw my arms around the appendage and hang on.

I suspect a real live dinosaur could have flung me off, but this machine's motions were not as flexible or vigorous as those of a living beast. It swung back and forth, but in a relatively smooth, predictable fashion, not curling or twisting. I found myself astride the metal column – and feeling the scales beneath my hands, there could be no doubt that they were metal – and I began slowly climbing up toward the monster's back.

Chapter Thirteen

In the Belly of the Beast

I was too concerned with my own situation to pay much attention to my companions or our three captives. I focused entirely on making my way up the creature's tail onto its back without being dislodged and flung aside. My fingers discovered joints in the metal where they could find purchase, which helped immensely, and for the first yard or so I was able to brace my feet on the curving spikes that protruded from either side of the tail's tip.

I reached the first of those strange plates for which the stegosaurus was famed. On the real animal they were bone, I suppose, perhaps covered with skin, but on this mechanical imitation they were unquestionably metal - *hot* metal, oddly enough, but metal. They provided very convenient handholds, and I was able to use them as a sort of ladder to climb upward.

Once I passed the point at which the tail was attached to the hips I was no longer in any danger of being flung aside; the thing's trunk was a solid mass of metal, with none of the flexibility of a living creature. It did sway slightly as the legs rose and fell, but it was no less stable than a walking horse, and I was able to proceed easily.

From this point on those metal plates were larger and even hotter to the touch. They seemed to vibrate under my fingers, and

I smelled something familiar, a blend of hot metal and smoke. I ignored that, looking for an opening as the monster thudded along the trail.

And sure enough, I found the hatch leading to the interior; it was concealed between the two rows of plates at the very peak of the monster's humped back, just ahead of its hips. The cover was secured with a simple latch that made no pretense of being anything else. I slid the latch open, lifted the metal panel, and stared down into the depths of the thing.

A roaring, grinding sound of working machinery billowed up, as if I had released it from its prison, and a rush of hot oily air swept across my face. The ticking we had heard before was now louder than any clock, but almost lost in the cacophony. I blinked and studied what I could see.

There was less space than I might have imagined, as most of the machine's interior seemed to be full of pipes, gears, belts, lockers, and moving shafts; any concerns we might have had about facing half a dozen crewmen were obviously unnecessary. It was all dimly lit by the red glow from a firebox almost directly below me, toward the rear, and two small oil lamps were mounted well forward of my position. A narrow ladder led down from where I perched.

The machinery was unfamiliar, but not so alien as to lend any great credence to the notion that it was the product of some lost civilization. While I had never seen such a collection before, the individual parts - pistons, valves, and the rest - were all things I had seen in various engines and workshops. I felt a slight twinge of disappointment.

I could see just two figures in that clanking, hissing, roaring gloom - one standing, shovel in hand, in front of that firebox, and the other seated amid dials and levers between the beast's front shoulders, his gaze fixed upon a large glass lens. A metal catwalk between them, perhaps seven or eight feet long, was the only other open space amid the machinery, and it was not so open as all that

- a tall man would need to stoop to walk on it.

The fireman looked up in horror at my arrival and dropped his shovel; I did not wait to see whether he had a weapon close at hand, but snatched my revolver from the holster on my belt and pointed it at him.

"Hands up!" I shouted – it was necessary to shout to be heard over the machinery.

The fireman flung his arms upward, banging one wrist on a black pipe and wincing in pain at the impact.

His face was black with soot, and his clothes, which consisted of a pair of canvas overalls over a shirt that might once have been white but was now a dark gray, were almost equally filthy. I had not immediately realized it, since the dim light and dirt so obscured his features, but he was scarcely more than a boy, probably younger than I was.

The engineer, as I assumed the other man in the machine to be, turned to look over his shoulder at me, but did not take his hands from the controls – nor his feet, for that matter, for I could see that he was working pedals as well as an assortment of levers and knobs.

I realized that he had completed his turning maneuver, and the contraption was now marching at a good speed back up the trail, toward the stockade. I swung my pistol over in his direction.

"Stop this thing!" I bellowed.

"I don't think so, Mister!" he shouted back. "And before you try to shoot me, think about where that bullet's going to go if you miss."

I hesitated, realizing that in fact, firing my weapon in so complex an enclosed space might be a very bad idea. The bullet would ricochet unpredictably. It might damage parts of the machinery, or find its way to either the fireman or myself. I straightened up, pulling my head out of the hatch, and looked back.

As best I could see in the lantern light, Betsy and Mr.

Cartwright seemed to have our three captives bound together, back to back to back. I knew from my training as an adventurer that that was not going to hold them for long; there were simply too many ways to bend and wiggle themselves until they found enough slack in the ropes to work themselves free. There was nothing I could do about it, though – I was atop a metal monster walking away from them at a steady pace that was about the speed of a healthy man's fast walk. The tail was no longer lashing, but instead dragged in the dirt, leaving that now familiar groove. Betsy and Mr. Cartwright were on their own.

Teddy Hancock, however, was pursuing the machine, his rifle in hand.

I put my hands around my mouth and called, "Mr. Hancock, if you want to see the insides of this thing, you better get up here quickly!"

With that, he broke into a run, gaining ground quickly.

I glanced down into the interior and saw that the fireman was still crouched in place, his hands up. However, the engineer, or operator, or whatever he called himself, was reaching for a wooden handle on the end of a long brass lever.

"Don't you touch that, or I *will* shoot, ricochet be damned!" I called, startling myself with my own use of profanity. I pointed the revolver in his general direction.

His hand withdrew, and from the corner of my eye I saw Teddy Hancock leap onto the thing's tail and begin climbing up toward me. A moment later he was crouched beside me atop the moving monstrosity.

"I'll cover you," I said. "You go down there and look around all you like."

"With those two both down there? Even with you covering me, one could jump me. If these really are Danites, they're fanatics willing to die for their cause."

I suppressed a sigh. I was beginning to get very tired of Mr. Hancock's obsession with Danites. I called down to the fireman,

"If you don't want to find yourself in even more trouble than you already are, you'll climb up out of this thing and go away."

"Yes, sir," he said. He reached for the ladder, then hesitated as Mr. Hancock also grabbed it. But then Mr. Hancock leaned back, and let the boy climb up.

"Bill, don't you go doing whatever they tell you..." the operator called, but the boy ignored him and hurried up the ladder.

It was a little awkward, squeezing him past us in the narrow space between the two rows of plates, but in a moment he was clambering awkwardly down the tail, and Mr. Hancock was swinging himself onto the ladder and descending quickly into the noisy, smoky gloom. I watched as Teddy maneuvered himself along the catwalk through the tangle of pipes and belts, coming up behind the operator's seat.

I had expected him to just look over the man's shoulder to study the controls and the machine's construction, but then he threw an arm around the engineer's neck.

"Now, my friend," he shouted over the noise, "you're going to get out of that seat and climb up the ladder. After that you're free to go; all I want, right now, is your machine."

"But it's not mine," the man protested. "It belongs to the church! You mustn't take it; it was built to defend the president!"

"Built," he had said. The possibility of an unknown civilization, or a relic from the Lost City, was now so faint as to be no longer worthy of consideration. Once again, I suppressed a sigh.

But I was young; I had my whole life to make great discoveries. And this machine was still an astonishing piece of work, even if it had been made by ordinary Americans.

Mr. Hancock glanced up at me, but in that moment of confusion and disappointment all I could do was shrug. "President Arthur?" he asked. "What does *he* have to do with any of this?"

"No, President *Taylor!*" the operator said, astonished. "The President of the Church of Jesus Christ of Latter-Day Saints!"

"Ha! I always *knew* it was Mormons!" This was hardly news, I thought, but perhaps Mr. Hancock had forgotten in his excitement what our captives had said about defending the church.

"Mr. H..." I called, intending to remind him that we had said we would not aid him in stealing the machine should it prove to be in the possession of its rightful owners. "Mr. H!"

Mr. Hancock ignored me as he shifted his grip, thrusting one arm under the engineer's arm and hoisting him bodily from his seat.

The machine gave a loud hiss as one hand released a lever. As the man's feet came off the pedals the creature's steady thudding walk began to slow. There was little room for the engineer to struggle – in fact, there was little room for any movement at all, and Mr. Hancock had to practically drag him up and over the back of his seat. The operator did thrash about a little, but only succeeded in clanging his boots and fists against various machinery as he was heaved up and back toward the ladder. I called a protest down into the creature's interior, but I doubt either man could hear me over all that racket. I dared not venture down to intervene; in so confined a space I could not be sure of doing any good, and might well damage something – or someone.

"The government in Washington is after him!" the man exclaimed, as he was hauled from his place. Mr. Hancock turned him to face the ladder, so I was able to hear him shout, "We've prepared a refuge, a place he can hide if they send troops to arrest him!"

"Is *that* what that stockade is?" I asked, fascinated, and distracted for a moment from Mr. Hancock's actions.

The engineer looked up at me and nodded. "The dinosaurs are to scare away anyone who gets too close!"

That cleared up *that* mystery, as well! It appeared we would not need to resort to any elaborate interrogations.

"Well, we don't give a tinker's dam about your president or his harem," Mr. Hancock told him, as he shoved him against the ladder. "You can have your refuge. I just came here for the dinosaurs."

"Come on up, mister," I said gently, extending a hand. "We aren't going to hurt any of you, but Mr. H. here is determined to have a good close look at one of your machines."

"I'm going to do more than look," Mr. Hancock said. "I'm taking this machine back to Ogden!"

"Mr. H, that's not..." I began.

"But that's *stealing!*" the engineer interrupted.

"Yes, it is," I agreed. "Mr. H, I thought we had agreed that we would not take it from its rightful owners."

"*You* agreed," Mr. Hancock replied. "*I* didn't. I came here to catch a dinosaur, and by God, I've caught this one and I'm not letting it go!"

I frowned. "Mr. H, please. This is not what we planned."

"It's what *I* planned, Derringer! The only way you'll get me out of here is if you shoot me."

I was unsure how to respond to that. Mr. Hancock had good reason to think I was not about to shoot him - although my agreement had been to bring him back dead or alive, I did not think my employers had considered the possibility that I might kill him. It was a safe bet that they would not look favorably on such an approach.

I thought for an instant that I might try to shoot him in such a way as to inflict a relatively minor wound, but in that dim, smoky interior I was not optimistic about my chances. If the truth be told, I was only a mediocre marksman.

No, I was not going to shoot him.

I struggled to find a fitting course of action. If we helped him steal the dinosaur, I told myself, perhaps we could seize some later opportunity to steal it back and return it to its owners. For now, though, I could not see any way to resolve the immediate situation peacefully other than assisting him.

"I'm afraid we *are* going to steal it," I told the engineer. I decided not to say anything about returning it, in case Mr. Hancock had better ears than I thought, but I did add, "Surely if you built this one, you can build more, can't you?"

"I don't think so," he said worriedly. "It was Elder Baldwin who built them, and I don't know that anyone else could duplicate his work."

I glanced over at Teddy. Unless the engineer was a superb and subtle liar, that settled the machine's origin beyond doubt. So much for lost civilizations or mysterious caverns. "Well, can't this Baldwin fellow build more?" I asked.

"Elder Baldwin died last winter, and it took him years to build the five we have."

That was another bit of information handed to us on a silver platter – there were exactly five dinosaurs. I knew enough engineering to know that any mechanism can be duplicated, even if doing so requires it to be taken apart, each piece copied, and then the entire thing reassembled, but I had to admit that recreating something like this machine without the aid of its designer would most likely be a great challenge. Hoping that Teddy would not realize I was serious, I said, "Well, maybe we'll bring it back when we're done with it, and in any case you'll still have the other four."

"But it's a secret! No outsiders are allowed to see it!"

I sighed in mild exasperation. "Mister," I said, "I am right here on top of your mysterious monster, and I have a Colt revolver pointed at your head." That was not literally true; I was aiming past his right ear, into the depths of the machinery. "I'd say the secret is out, and do you *really* think this is a good time to argue with me? Now, get up here and get out!"

The creature had come to a standstill, though I could still hear clicking, whirring, ticking, huffing, and other noises from the various internal mechanisms, and various gears and shafts were still turning. The engineer looked around at his machine, then shrugged. "You'll never be able to operate it," he said. "And even if you could, without Bill shoveling coal you wouldn't be able to get very far anyway."

"You just tell yourself that," Mr. Hancock said, heaving the engineer up the ladder by the back of his coat. "Now, get!"

I moved aside, and the engineer got, climbing quickly past me. Rather than climbing down the tail, as I had expected, he swung himself over one line of metal plates and skidded down the scaled flank, dropping the final five or six feet to the ground. He landed on his feet but tumbled forward, then quickly straightened up and broke into a run. I watched him vanish up the trail into the darkness, in the direction of the enclosure.

And that left Mr. Hancock and myself in complete command of the Stegosaurus. "Well," I said, "why don't you take a seat there, Mr. Hancock, and let us see if you can drive this oversized clockwork back to Ogden."

"With pleasure," Hancock replied. He clambered forward, slid into the operator's metal chair, and began studying the controls.

I waited for him to start pulling levers, and for the machine to resume walking, but nothing happened. After a long moment I heard him say quietly, "Damme."

"What is it?" I asked.

"That pipsqueak was right," Hancock replied. "I haven't the first notion of how to work this thing. The gauges are in English, but I don't know what half the terms and abbreviations mean. None of the controls are labeled, and I don't want to just start tugging them at random."

I frowned. "I'd assumed you knew something about this," I said.

He shook his head. "I'm an adventurer," he said, "so I know a great many odd things, but I am *not* an engineer, and I can't make head nor tail of this. I thought there'd be a lever or two, not whole racks of them, and not a one of them has any indication what it's for!"

That left us in a potentially awkward position. "Maybe we had best abandon it. I know you wanted to take it back to Ogden..."

"I am *not* giving up!" he bellowed over the machinery. "If I can't do it any other way, I'm going to just start pulling levers until I figure them out."

"That could be dangerous," I said. I gestured at the various pipes and gauges, at hissing valves and at needles inching to one side or the other.

"You can go if you want."

I was no more inclined to give up Mr. Hancock than he was to give up the Stegosaurus. I thought I might be able to overpower him, but I was not at all sure, and that would almost certainly mean dragging him back to Ogden as my prisoner. I was no bounty hunter, and he was not a wanted criminal; I had no legal authority to take him prisoner.

Perhaps if we could figure out the controls, we could find some limitation that would prevent him from taking the machine very far. After all, he had told us he never saw one travel more than a mile or two; perhaps they couldn't. If they were only meant to defend that refuge, they would not need much range.

I had no more idea of how to operate the thing than he did, but we *did* have an engineer in our party. I stood up over the hatch, cupped my hands around my mouth, and shouted into the night as loudly as I could, "Betsy! We need a hand here!"

"I'll be right there!" she called back. Her voice was faint; apparently we had covered more ground than I had realized before bringing the machine to a halt.

A moment later she appeared, lantern in hand. "Climb up the tail!" I called.

Then I saw that her other hand held the rifle I had dropped.

"Oh, good girl!" I said, and immediately hoped that had not sounded as patronizing as I feared it did. I tried to distract her by continuing, "We can't figure out the controls. I thought you might have better luck at it, with your background in mechanics."

She paused to sling the rifle on her back and to adjust her hold on the lantern. "I'll take a look," she said; then she tucked up her skirts and began climbing the tail. Now that the machine was standing motionless it was not a particularly difficult ascent, and a moment later I had shifted to the forward side of the hatch and was giving her a hand to guide her onto the ladder.

"Wait a minute," she said. She knelt atop the metal spine long enough to take the rifle from her back and hand it to me, followed by the lantern; then she scrambled down into the machine as easily as a squirrel runs down a tree.

I peered down into the gloomy interior to watch as Mr. Hancock reluctantly yielded his place to her, barely able to squeeze past her on the catwalk without committing an affront. "D'you really think you can run this thing, Miss Vanderhart?" he asked.

"I don't know," she said, looking around. Her eyes followed first one shaft or pipe, then another, and then she plopped herself into the operator's chair and bent over one of the gauges.

"Steam pressure's dropping," she said, tapping the dial's glass cover. "Someone needs to feed the boiler."

"Then it's all powered by steam?" I asked.

"Oh, of course it is," she replied. "What else could move something this size?"

"It sounds like clockwork," I replied.

"Well, there's plenty of gearing, and I'd say there are some pretty sophisticated regulators," she said, "but the motive power is steam." She rapped a pipe with her knuckle. "Right here's the pressure line for the right front foot, and over there's the left, and from the look of that linkage..." She did not finish the sentence, but instead stepped on one of the pedals, turning a valve as she did so.

The mechanical beast came to life once again; I could feel its balance shift as it lifted a forefoot from the ground. Betsy shoved a two-foot lever forward, then stepped on the other pedal.

The entire contraption swayed unsteadily and lurched forward.

"Oops," Betsy said, working both pedals rhythmically. The machine righted itself, having apparently moved forward perhaps six inches. "I'll need a few minutes to get the hang of it."

"We need to turn it around," I said. "It's pointed at the Saints' stockade, and we want to take it toward Ogden."

"We do? Oh, of course we do." She studied the levers, then peered into that big lens. "Oh, this is clever," she said. "There's a viewer here, I think it's a system of mirrors, with a peephole in the thing's mouth. I can see where we're going. Or I could if it wasn't so dark."

"In its mouth?" Hancock asked. "Not its eyes?"

"Definitely not its eyes," Betsy said, staring at the glass. "Pretty sure it's the mouth." She chose a lever at one side – I have no idea whether she had a solid reason for her selection, or was choosing at random, but when she pulled it the thing raised its head. The motion attracted my eye, and I turned to watch.

The head swung around to one side, then back to the other, and after some adjustment once again pointed straight ahead. With a hiss, the Stegosaurus began walking, very slowly, stepping with one foot at a time – left rear, right fore, right rear, left fore.

"Get us turned around!" I called down the hatch. "We're still heading toward the stockade, and those two boys we threw out of here are going for reinforcements, sure as my name is Derringer!"

"Give me a moment," she called. Then she turned and spoke over her shoulder. "And I could use more pressure, if one of you could stoke the fire back there."

"I'll do it," Mr. Hancock said. He peeled off his sheepskin vest, tossed his battered bowler aside, rolled up his sleeves, and took up the fireman's shovel.

Chapter Fourteen

A Wild Ride

It took about ten minutes of experimentation before Betsy finally managed to turn the dinosaur aside, rather than continuing in a straight line, and that first success was a mixed blessing, as we promptly stamped off the trail, crushing a clump of antelope brush. She was able to swerve before we struck anything larger, and managed to bring us safely to a halt. We paused, with Mr. Hancock shoveling coal from one of the lockers into the firebox, as she puzzled out her next step. At last she arrived at a solution and was able to back us out of the thicket and onto the trail – and then we continued off the other side. I shouted a warning down to her, and she was able to stop before we collided with anything that might damage our stolen machine.

"I can't see anything that direction," she protested.

"I know," I said, shouting down into the machine from my perch on the rim of the hatch. "I'm not criticizing, Betsy, I swear I'm not. I think you're doing brilliantly. I'll do my best to guide you until we get headed the right direction."

"Even when we *are* headed the right way, I won't be able to see much," she said. "It's *dark* out there."

"Hold on," I said. "Don't move anything for a moment."

"What are you..." she began, but I did not wait to hear the end of her sentence; I was hurrying down the thing's spine, not toward its tail this time, but toward its head. I stretched myself out across that barrel-shaped protrusion, looking for somewhere I could hang the lantern.

In the end I had to do considerable stretching and came very close to falling off – which would not have been fatal, by any means, but it *would* have been uncomfortable and inconvenient. At last, though, I managed to stay on board while hanging the lantern from one of the monster's teeth.

The teeth, I might add, appeared to be made of carved bone, rather than metal, in a surprising bit of authenticity.

Once the lantern was secure I scrambled back up to the hatch and called down, "How's that?"

"Better," Betsy replied. "Much better. I still can't see very far, but it's considerably farther than before. Thank you, Tom."

I felt a rush of warmth at her words, but I did not let that distract me; I seated myself on the edge of the hatchway, rifle in my arms, watching for any sign of trouble. As I settled into position the machine gave a lurch, swung its head to one side, and then began moving again, this time finally turning to head down the trail *away* from the stockade.

Betsy quickly found a rhythm, and the machine began to pick up speed, resuming the steady thudding that we had heard before our ambush – perhaps not *quite* as fast, but still moving at a respectable pace.

It was several minutes before I glimpsed another light, well ahead of us. I hoped that this was Mr. Cartwright's lantern, and that our three captives had not yet escaped, or that some new party had not joined in.

I was not disappointed in those hopes. At the sight of the approaching monster Cartwright raised a rifle, but he hesitated, clearly unsure what the significance might be of the lantern hanging from the creature's jaw. And then he saw me sitting atop the beast, waving to him. He let the barrel of his weapon droop.

"It's us, Mr. Cartwright," I called.

I could not hear his reply over the noise of the machine, but I could imagine it. He lowered his rifle and waved, then glanced back over his shoulder; I guessed he was checking on the prisoners.

A moment later we came stamping up to him, and I called down to Betsy to stop, only to see that she was already pushing levers back into resting position and lifting her feet from the pedals.

Cartwright came up alongside the mechanical beast and called up, "Congratulations, Mr. Derringer! Where are the others?"

"Miss Vanderhart is steering this thing, while Mr. Hancock stokes its fires – it takes two people to run it, and there's scarcely room in there for more. What's your own situation?"

"I've been keeping an eye on the three rascals we tied up, and I took the opportunity to ask them a few questions. I've also made sure the mules are ready to go on a moment's notice."

"Excellent!" I glanced down into the interior, where Mr. Hancock was looking up at me. I looked back to Mr. Cartwright. "It's Mr. Hancock's intention to drive this contraption back down to Ogden as quickly as we can, and I have not been able to dissuade him. We sent its original crew on their way, and I'll wager they headed straight back to that enclosure of theirs. I think we can expect pursuit in fairly short order, so we need all the head start we can get. If you can manage all four of the mules, I'd appreciate it if you could accompany us – on mule-back or on foot, whichever you please."

He nodded. "What about the prisoners?"

"Set 'em free, I'd say, so long as you make sure they aren't armed. It's not as if we can keep what we're doing secret any more."

"Fair enough."

"You can tell me about what they said once we're well on our way."

He nodded, and headed in the direction of our camp, where

the mules had presumably slept through all the excitement. I leaned over and called down, "How are you doing in there?"

"I'm fine," Betsy replied. "Just admiring some of the craftsmanship here. It may not have been built by subterranean scientists or the like, but it's really an amazing feat of engineering, Tom! There's a system to pull in air with a bellows in each leg joint, so we don't smother, and the gearing is just brilliant."

"I'm glad to hear it," I said. "What about you, Mr. Hancock?"

"I'm holding up well enough," he said, wiping his brow with a dirty handkerchief. "It's *hot* in here, though, and I hadn't used a shovel much of late. It's a safe bet my arms will be sore tomorrow."

"He's doing a good job keeping the pressure up," Betsy remarked.

I could tell it was hot down inside the machine; the metal where I sat was hot, as well, and heat billowed up through the hatch as if it was the door of a furnace. I knew the night air around me was chilly, but I was no longer feeling any of that.

"Well, pace yourself, Mr. Hancock," I said. "It's a long way to Ogden." I hesitated, then suggested, "If you've reconsidered, we could leave the machine here with the prisoners..."

"Never!" he exclaimed. "I risked my life to get this thing, and I am not giving it up."

I could see Betsy eyeing me from the pilot's seat, but I was unsure just what she thought of our situation. I would need to discuss it with her when we had a chance to do so without Mr. Hancock within earshot.

"If you insist, Mr. Hancock, but then you can't complain about the conditions."

He grimaced, then asked, "Pete's all right, out there? I couldn't hear half of what you said."

"He's fine," I assured him. "He's fetching the mules."

"Good!" he replied. "No sense leaving them up here for the

Danites."

I hesitated, then told him, "It's not just that. It really is a long way to Ogden, over more than a few mountains, and I'm not sure this machine can make it." I did not mention that I did not want it to make it. "We may need those mules ourselves if this thing breaks down."

"Or if the coal or water runs out," Betsy added. "It won't run on air."

"We can find water," Mr. Hancock protested.

"But we can't find coal," I said. "She's right about that. I don't know how much is in those lockers around you, but we aren't going to have any more when it's gone. And much as I admire Betsy's mechanical skills, I admit to doubts about her ability to repair this should it break down."

"I don't have my tools," Betsy confirmed.

"There's a toolbox back here," Mr. Hancock pointed out.

"There is?" Betsy twisted around to get a better look. "Then we might be all right, while the coal holds out. *If* it holds out."

"Shouldn't we get moving, then?" Hancock asked. "Pete can catch up."

"Tom?"

I looked around, then shrugged. "Not too fast," I said.

Betsy reached out, spun a valve, then stepped on the pedals, and the Stegosaurus whirred, clanked, and began walking again.

"I see those Mormons," she called.

I looked ahead and saw the three men, tied back to back, on the side of the path ahead. "Don't step on them," I answered.

"Maybe someone should move them," she said uncertainly.

I looked at our course, and at the men, and said, "I'll take care of it." I set my rifle down on the creature's back, tucked securely at the base of the left-hand spinal plates, then called down, "Don't move the tail!"

"I haven't yet figured out *how* to move the tail!"

"Well, this would be a bad time to find out," I said. Then I stepped over the right-hand plates in the same fashion I had seen the machine's original pilot employ, slid down the side, and dropped to the ground.

I had thought I would be able to take the impact with my knees and remain on my feet, but I did not manage that feat any more than the engineer had; instead I fell forward and turned my fall into a forward roll. I then sprang up and trotted to the prisoners.

"Mr. C. took your guns?" I asked.

"Yes, sir," the youngest of them replied.

I had been thinking I might free them on the spot, but I found that Mr. Cartwright had done a better job than I expected; the knots were pulled tight, and the ropes wound both over and under their arms. I glanced back at the approaching behemoth and decided to take the simplest path to a solution; I grabbed one man's legs and up-ended him, sending the entire threesome tumbling off the trail and under a scrubby shrub – an evergreen of some sort, but not one I could identify in the dark.

"You should be able to work yourselves free soon enough," I said. "Go ahead and yell, if you like; we don't mind. Your two friends who were driving the dinosaur are on their way back to the stockade, and I expect someone will be along to give you a hand before long."

All three started to protest, but I paid them no mind as I turned and ran back past the machine, then turned again and grabbed the tail as it passed. A moment later I was back in my perch atop its back, rifle in hand, and we were marching our way past the three captives.

I watched to see whether they were making any progress in disentangling themselves, but then a sound drew my attention, even over the thumping of the immense metal feet, and I saw Mr. Cartwright, lantern in hand, leading a line of mules out of the brush. "Hallo!" I called, with a wave. Then I bent over the hatch. "We're all here, Betsy," I called. "You can speed up a little. Try not to go too fast for the mules, though – they have all our supplies."

"How am I supposed to know how fast those confounded mules are?" she asked, but she heaved on two of the largest levers and stamped on two pedals, and our conveyance began to pick up speed, swaying and thumping vigorously down the trail.

We marched on, with Mr. Cartwright and the string of mules following behind.

It was perhaps half an hour later that we came to the end of the trail, and Betsy brought the beast to a stop. After a little experimentation she swung the immense head from side to side, setting the lantern to swinging wildly, then asked, "Which way now?"

I looked out into the gloom of the mountain night. The trail had left us in a broad open area, and I did not recognize anything within reach of the lantern's glow. I looked up at the sky, but clouds hid the constellations I had hoped might guide me. I knew we were four or five days past the new moon, and I estimated it was roughly midnight, or a little after, so the moon's crescent should be low in the western sky – or southwestern, really. I had not paid as much attention to my astronomical training as I should have, and was unable to calculate the correct angle for our present date and location, but I knew the moon would be somewhere between due west and due south. I also knew we wanted to head more or less southwest. I searched the sky.

The moon was behind the clouds and less than half full, but I could nonetheless make out enough of its light to approximate its position, and with that information I made my best guess as to where our intended course lay. "Bear right, up over that ridge," I said.

"Are you sure?"

"No," I admitted. "But do you have a better idea?"

Mr. Hancock burst out, "Is this some sort of trick, Derringer? Are you telling me you don't know how to get back to Ogden?"

"Not exactly, no," I replied. "I know it's to the southwest, and by daylight I might recognize some landmarks, but it's the middle of the night, it's cloudy, and I can't see much beyond the lantern's light."

"Maybe we should stop until daylight," Betsy said. "Mr. Hancock must be getting tired of wielding that shovel, and I'm not entirely fresh myself."

"We're not stopping yet, even if my arms are sore," Mr. Hancock said. "I don't think those Mormons will wait until dawn to come after us."

"Well, they can't see well enough to follow us in the dark, any more than we can see our way!" I argued.

"Mr. Derringer," he replied, "we are riding a very large and distinctive vehicle that leaves large and distinctive tracks and makes loud and distinctive noises, and what's more, it's a vehicle which I'll wager they very badly want back. I have been looking over Miss Vanderhart's shoulder at that viewing mechanism, and it appears we are in open country and have done nothing to disguise our trail. I think they can find us if we stay here."

"If I take us across bare stone it won't leave tracks," Betsy said. "And if we shut down the engine for the rest of the night once we're away from here, they won't be able to hear us."

I considered our situation. I did want to give the Stegosaurus back to those Latter-Day Saints, but I knew our own interests would best be served if we were not with it when they found it, so getting away from this trail head did seem advisable.

"That's a good idea," I said. I peered around, trying to make out as much as I could in the sparse light of lantern, moon, and stars. "We *still* want to go over that ridge, though."

Betsy nodded and turned the contraption's steps in that direction.

I would estimate that we continued for almost an hour more before driving the Stegosaurus into a sheltered corner beneath a cliff and shutting down the machinery. Drooping tree branches largely hid it from sight. Mr. Hancock did his best to bank the fires so that we would not need to start cold in the morning, while Mr. Cartwright and I set up camp perhaps fifty yards away, on the other side of a line of trees.

And that done, the four of us collapsed into our bedding, exhausted. I had debated with myself whether we should post a guard, but in the end I simply couldn't be bothered. If the Saints found us I had little doubt they would arrive in sufficient numbers to completely overwhelm any defense we might make; our only hope of success was to avoid discovery. If they found their prized machine unguarded, they might well assume we had abandoned it and fled; I hoped they would be satisfied with its return and would not bother to pursue us.

I lay down with my rifle close at hand, took one final look around, and then closed my eyes and descended instantly into sleep.

Chapter Fifteen

Flight!

The sun was well up the eastern sky when we awoke, and there was as yet no sign of pursuit; apparently our attempts to disguise our route had succeeded.

I would have preferred to have simply mounted up on our mules and headed for Ogden, but Mr. Hancock would still not hear of it; if Betsy and I would not assist him in getting the dinosaur back to civilization, he would try to drive it himself. He had been watching Betsy for hours, and thought he could probably manage. He would need to stop frequently to feed the boiler, of course, if he was trying to operate it single-handed.

I did not know whether he could indeed pilot it safely, but it did not really matter; I was not going to leave him by himself. I had said I would do everything I could to bring him back, and I would. Abandoning him out here with this contraption was not an acceptable course of action. Even if he did not manage to kill himself somehow by pulling the wrong lever or turning the wrong valve, the odds were excellent that he would be captured by the Saints – captured, or killed.

Short of violence I did not see any way to pry him away from that confounded machine, so I really did not think that we had any choice but to continue on toward Ogden as a group, with the Stegosaurus, as quickly as we could. Even as we argued, therefore, we ate a hasty cold breakfast from our dwindling supplies and prepared to depart.

All four of us discussed our situation while we ate, however, not just Teddy and myself. I was interested to hear what Mr. Cartwright had learned from the three men we had captured. I had known, of course, that our national government in Washington did not approve of the Mormon faith, and most particularly did not approve of their custom of plural marriage, where one man would take several wives. Congress had outlawed the practice – twice, in fact – in all U.S. territories not yet admitted to statehood, first with the Morrill Act in 1862, and much more recently with the Edmunds Act of 1882, which made bigamous or polygamous marriage, or even cohabitation, a felony, as Mr. Cartwright had told us before. This had a calamitous effect on the elders of the Church of Jesus Christ of Latter-Day Saints, several of whom had been arrested and imprisoned.

That much I had known, though I had never given it a great deal of thought.

What I had *not* known was that John Taylor, the president of the church, had eight wives and had been forced by the Edmunds Act to abandon all of them – he had refused to favor any one of them over the other seven and had instead moved in with his sister, Agnes. Much of the congregation assumed that this would not be sufficient to deter the territorial government, and that at any moment federal marshals might come to arrest the man that most of the Latter-Day Saints revered as God's representative on Earth, someone they considered a possible prophet. His predecessors, Joseph Smith and Brigham Young, had been declared prophets; President Taylor had not yet assumed that title, but many felt it was his by right.

His arrest, it was thought, might spark an outright religious war. The Latter-Day Saints had engaged in open warfare with their neighbors and with federal authorities more than once in their history, and the possibility that it might once again come to that could not be dismissed out of hand.

At this point in the conversation Mr. Hancock began ranting about imagined Danite atrocities, to Mr. Cartwright's obvious discomfort, but eventually Betsy and I managed to quiet him sufficiently to hear the rest of Mr. Cartwright's explanations.

A group of Mormon gentlemen had taken it upon themselves to prepare for the eventuality of an attempt to arrest President Taylor and had built a refuge in the wilderness, with the idea that President Taylor could hide out there, and continue to preside over the church from exile until such time as the federal government came to its senses.

That was Mr. Cartwright's phrase, "comes to its senses." Neither Betsy nor Mr. Hancock seemed to think it an appropriate way to put it. I could see how the idea of plural marriage might be repulsive to a respectable young woman, but why Teddy Hancock, who had adventured in foreign lands where such things were generally accepted, should be so adamantly opposed, I did not entirely see. Perhaps it was the notion that so barbarous a practice could exist among his own supposedly modern and civilized people.

At any rate, that explained the stockade and the enclosure behind it; it was the refuge these men had prepared against the day their beloved leader might need to flee Salt Lake City.

And the dinosaurs? Our captives had told Mr. Cartwright that those were the work of an eccentric engineer by the name of Nehemiah Baldwin. He had intended them as a part of the defenses that would protect President Taylor, should he be forced into exile. Elder Baldwin had at one time been in the employ of Professor Othniel Charles Marsh, Yale's famous paleontologist, in Dr. Marsh's studies of the western fossil beds, so he was quite familiar with the known history of the Stegosaurus and had thought that such a creature would serve as a serious deterrent to anyone seeking to pursue President Taylor.

He had hoped that his creations would be sufficiently lifelike to fool observers into thinking that his fellows had captured and trained actual living dinosaurs, but in the end he had realized that they were not as convincing as he had hoped. At night they could be reasonably effective in maintaining the desired illusion, but in the light of day, Mr. Cartwright had been told, they would not fool anyone – certainly not at any distance less than a hundred feet.

Still, the little group of President Taylor's would-be defenders had helped Elder Baldwin to build and maintain a total of five of these monstrous machines, in hopes they might discourage any federal troops that approached their refuge. They were not happy that anyone had observed them, as the entire project was intended to remain secret for the present.

And they would be even less happy that one of the five machines had been stolen.

"Well, they'll just have to live with it," Mr. Hancock replied. "I don't plan to give it back."

I was not particularly pleased with his attitude. These people had built the machines themselves; they had not stolen them, despite Mr. Hancock's theories. I did not say anything more just then, though. Any argument could serve no useful purpose in the face of his resolution. Mr. Hancock might not intend to give it back, but *I* did; still, I could not see any reason to debate the question just then.

"I think they may be just as concerned that we'll tell the territorial government where their refuge is," Mr. Cartwright replied.

"I don't care one way or the other about that," Mr. Hancock said.

"I don't see any reason we should make trouble for the Saints," I said. "It seems to me that Mr. Taylor is doing what he can to abide by the law."

"The man held *eight women* in bondage!" Betsy protested.

Mr. Cartwright expostulated, "*Bondage*! He married them honorably and supported them as best he could!"

"I don't see anything honorable in abducting eight women!"

"He didn't abduct anybody!"

By this time we had finished our meal; I got to my feet, dusted off a few crumbs, and said, "Let us table this discussion for the present. If we really are going to drive that thing to Ogden, I think we must get moving."

No one argued with that. Mr. Cartwright turned to tend to the mules, while Betsy and I headed for the concealed machine.

Mr. Hancock hung back. I turned. I had initially assumed that we would take on the same roles as we had the previous night, but it seemed Mr. Hancock objected.

"I think it's time someone else took a turn shoveling coal," he said. "My arms are aching."

I reluctantly conceded that he had a fair point. Obviously, Betsy would continue as our machine's operator, since neither Mr. Cartwright nor I had the faintest idea how it worked and we could not spare the time for instruction, and I did not trust Mr. Hancock to have learned as much from observing Betsy as he thought he had. Besides, while she was a remarkable young woman, she was simply too small to handle the shovel effectively, and she still had no fondness for the mules.

The three of us men, though, were more or less interchangeable – or so I would have thought, but Mr. Cartwright insisted he wanted nothing to do with that machine and would happily continue as our teamster the entire way to Ogden.

I, therefore, was elected to take on the role of fireman, and with a sigh I made my way to the niche where the lifeless monster waited, to get the fires blazing and build up steam while Betsy finished her breakfast and helped break camp.

As I rounded the rocky outcropping and passed the sheltering trees, I got my first good look at the thing in daylight. Until that moment I had not realized just how *shiny* it was, but even where it stood partly shaded by rock and trees it gleamed in the morning sun as brightly as a new penny. If its metal scales were not pure copper, they were surely close.

It was no wonder, I thought, that its creators had only ever taken it out at night. On open ground, in daylight, that thing would be visible for *miles*.

And we were about to take it out on the road to Ogden on a bright sunny day. Yes, our path would lead through trees and valleys, but it was not as sheltered as all that. I hesitated, chewing my lower lip. Should we perhaps wait until nightfall?

No, I decided, that would merely give our assumed pursuers more time to find us. Our best chance of staying away from them, I thought, lay in speed. I fully expected to find some opportunity to abandon the thing, despite Mr. Hancock's determination, and when we did I wanted to be well away from it before its owners retrieved it. That resolved, at least to my satisfaction, I climbed up the monster's back, and then down the ladder into the dark interior of its belly.

I had not realized until then just how dirty and malodorous that interior was. Hancock's clothes had *already* been tattered and filthy when he took up the shovel, so the additional layer of soot and the added smells had not been especially noticeable. Experiencing the conditions firsthand, though, was another matter. The mechanism stank of coal smoke and machine oil, and everything was covered in a fine layer of gritty black dust that was far more visible in the weak daylight spilling through the hatch than it had ever been in the red glow of the firebox.

I found the coal locker, which was still roughly half full, and the water reserve that had to be fed into the boiler through a complicated system of valves whenever the steam pressure dropped. There were fairly straightforward gauges to keep track of the current status – temperature, pressure, and water level. I did not know how fast we would be using the water, but the tanks appeared to be somewhat more than half full. We would do well to top them off at the first opportunity, I thought, but our campsite did not have a water source; we had relied on our canteens.

There was a device that sifted coal ash out of the firebox into a tray, and I observed that the tray was full, almost overflowing. I found a lever that opened a narrow vent at the back and allowed the ash to spill out between the dinosaur's rear legs, and I proceeded to empty out as much ash as I readily could.

We had never seen deposits of such ash along the trail; I supposed the Saints had only emptied the ash box inside their stockade, so as not to attract the notice of passing wanderers.

Last night's coals were still dimly glowing in the bottom of the firebox, and I adjusted the dampers to let in more air before clearing away ash and adding fresh coal – the controls for *this* operation were familiar enough that I could manage this unassisted. I pumped more water into the boiler and set about building up steam. A brass governor above the firebox began to turn, and then to spin, faster and faster until it was a golden blur.

It occurred to me that the smoke and steam this machine generated must be going somewhere, but I did not know where; they seemed to simply vanish into the tangle of pipes above the firebox. I reminded myself to ask Betsy about this when the opportunity arose.

And as if my thought had summoned her a shadow appeared in the hatchway above me, and Betsy climbed down the ladder.

"It smells even worse in here than it did last night," she said, wrinkling her nose. "I didn't say anything because it wasn't important, and I thought some of it might just be Teddy Hancock, but this thing really does stink."

I could not argue. "I was wondering," I said, "where the coal smoke goes."

"I have no idea," she said, as she squeezed around and slid into the operator's seat. "The firebox is vented into that system of pipes right there," she added, pointing to something overhead, "but where those go, I don't know. Last night I was more concerned with learning the controls." She leaned forward and studied a set of gauges. "We should be ready to go in a minute or two."

"Where's Mr. Hancock?" I asked. "Will he be riding up top, as I did?"

Betsy shrugged. "I'm not sure whether he plans to ride shotgun with us, or handle two of the mules. And to be honest, Tom, I don't much care. I'm starting us up when we're ready whether he's up there or not."

"Betsy, the only reason we're taking this thing is to get Teddy to Ogden. Leaving him behind out here will defeat the whole purpose. If I thought we could safely return this to its owners and still get Teddy to come with us, I would."

"Well, if we did get the machine away from him we could give it back to the Mormons, but I don't think he'll ever let that happen. And I'd rather drive this thing than ride a mule, anyway."

"Despite the smell?"

"I don't much care for the smell of mule, either."

I was not inclined to argue further. I glanced up at the open hatch, debating whether to close it or leave it as it was.

"Hey, in there!" Mr. Hancock's voice called, barely audible over the popping and hissing as the machine built up a head of steam.

I put down the shovel and took a few steps up the ladder, peering between two of the spinal plates at him. He was standing perhaps thirty feet away, waving his battered bowler. "What is it?" I shouted back.

"Something's on fire!"

I had no idea what he was talking about, so I climbed further up the ladder, and then I saw.

Pale gray smoke was rising all around the hatch, and in fact all along the dinosaur's back, from neck to hip. I looked more closely at some of the nearest streams and realized that each of the metal plates that were arranged in two rows along the creature's spine had a small pipe running up through its center, and that smoke was spilling from every one of these vents.

That answered my earlier question of where the coal smoke went. Rather than a single plume from a smokestack, such as a locomotive would have, this thing produced dozens of smaller streams. I supposed that was so that it would be less obvious that it was a machine, and not a live animal. This also explained why those plates had been so warm to the touch.

None of that smoke had been visible in the dark when we first encountered the contraption; if we *had* seen it, we would most probably have assumed it to be night mist.

By daylight, however, the smoke was definitely visible. Combined with the bright exterior, the thing would be *very* visible, even from a considerable distance.

For a moment I debated anew whether perhaps we should therefore travel only at night, but then I dismissed the notion; it was entirely possible our pursuers, if we actually had any, had *already* seen the smoke and had thereby already discerned our approximate whereabouts.

"We need to get going," I told Betsy. "Smoke is venting out through the spinal plates and must be visible for miles. We'll need to rely on speed to get to Ogden before we're caught."

"If I go *too* fast, Mr. Cartwright won't be able to keep up."

"Can this thing *go* that fast?"

"If the path is good enough, yes, I think it can. I was only running about half speed most of last night."

"Then let's see what this machine can do." I slid back down the ladder and reached for the shovel, and Betsy grabbed the two largest levers and hauled them all the way back.

With a clank something slipped into place, that confounded ticking resumed, and the machine began moving, swaying a little more than it had the night before. I could feel that we were turning, but could see nothing of the outside world, just my own little station. I checked the gauges, scooped up a shovelful of coal, and resumed feeding the fire.

The familiar thudding joined the machinery's other sounds

and quickly picked up speed.

"Do you know the way?" I called.

"I'm taking my bearings from the sun," she replied. "It's simple enough."

"Good!" I hesitated, then added, "If you see a good water source, we should probably fill the tanks."

"Good idea, Tom. I'll keep an eye out."

After that we did not bother with conversation for quite some time. Mr. Hancock never did appear at the hatch above us, and we assumed that he had chosen to stay with the mules and Mr. Cartwright. I fervently hoped that we had not lost him, while at the same time I wondered whether we might now be able to abandon the Stegosaurus.

If we did, though, Teddy would probably do his best to reclaim it before the Saints could. I put aside the idea for the moment.

The sun had neared its zenith when out of nowhere Betsy asked, "Do you really think all eight of those women married John Taylor willingly?"

"I have no reason to think otherwise," I said, putting down the coal shovel for a moment to wipe my brow. "Strange as it may seem to *us*, polygamy is a widespread practice in the world, and the Saints have followed it for half a century. These women probably grew up thinking it entirely natural; indeed, their own fathers may well have had multiple wives."

"It's disgusting."

I shrugged. "I can't say I see the appeal myself." (I confess this was not *entirely* true, but on balance I thought the drawbacks very much outweighed the benefits.)

"They can't have all been in *love* with him."

"Not everyone marries for love, you know – not among the Saints, nor anywhere else."

"I suppose not," she admitted, as the mechanical monster swayed; we were traversing a narrow mountain pass where there was no smooth trail of a size to accommodate our vehicle. "But it still..."

She stopped in mid-sentence, listening. "Did you hear something?" she asked.

"No," I said.

"I thought I did. Could you climb up and take a look?"

I was glad to have an excuse to put the shovel down again – and also, though I had not yet said anything about it to Betsy, to avoid looking into the coal locker, because it was becoming plain to me that unless I had badly misjudged our rate of travel, we would run out of fuel while still well short of our destination. Water we could expect to find, but coal, we could not.

I did want to abandon the dinosaur eventually and let its rightful owners recover it, but I wanted to choose the place, and be sure we were well clear before they arrived, rather than allow ourselves to be stranded somewhere at random. If the coal ran out while we were in a confined area somewhere that might be awkward.

I climbed up the ladder and thrust my head out through the hatch. To either side I could see nothing yet but the creature's metal plates, streaming smoke; ahead of us I saw only the trail through the mountains.

Behind us, though, I saw Teddy Hancock riding toward us, holding onto his galloping mule's reins with one hand while he waved his bowler in the air with his other. He was shouting, and though I could not make out his words, there could be no question that he wanted to bring something urgent to our attention.

"It's Mr. Hancock," I called down to Betsy. "You'd better slow down, so we can find out what's happening."

"Yes, Tom," she said, and she shoved two levers forward.

Chapter Sixteen

Pursuit!

As the contraption slowed, Mr. Hancock swiftly gained ground. I had expected him to dismount and climb the tail, but instead he rode up alongside and shouted, "They're coming! All of 'em! They're following your smoke!"

"All of them?" I asked. "What do you mean, all of them?"

"The other dinosaurs! All four of them are after you!"

That was not what I had expected. I had assumed that a party of armed men would come after us; I had not anticipated a party of mechanical dinosaurs. I found myself puzzled; what did they hope to accomplish with these machines? Ours did not have any weaponry built into it, or at least none that Betsy had detected during her inspections; were the others armed in some fashion? In any case, unleashing the entire herd against us would hardly help to keep their existence secret!

"What about you?" I called back. "What about Mr. Cartwright?"

"I reckon they want their machine back!" Mr. Hancock replied. "They haven't...Pete's hiding. He has the other three mules and all the packs, and he's gone into hiding. He reckons those things won't bother looking for him; they want their dinosaur. I took the fastest mule to come warn you."

"Thank you!"

"What..." He seemed to be having some difficulty in phrasing his next question.

I had to duck just then to avoid an overhanging tree branch; it missed me and scraped along the left-hand row of plates. When we were past I looked down at Mr. Hancock again. "Go on to Ogden!" I told him. "We'll deal with them!"

"The devil you will! That's *my* dinosaur!"

I had no idea what to say to that. In fact, my plan had been to abandon the machine at some opportune time and tell Mr. Hancock we had run out of coal, whether we had or not, but apparently that was not going to work.

I silently cursed myself for not having *already* abandoned the machine while we were out of Mr. Hancock's sight. I could have dumped the remaining coal over the side. I had missed my chance; I could not dispose of it while he was in sight.

"I'm coming aboard!" he shouted.

"What? I don't..." I did not bother to finish my sentence; he was galloping up ahead, out of earshot.

"Should I speed up again?" Betsy called.

"No!" I shouted down to her. "Just...hold on." Ahead of us Mr. Hancock reined in his mount and swung himself out of the saddle, letting the mule free. The animal promptly wandered off, reins dragging the ground, in search of provender.

Meanwhile, Mr. Hancock was waiting for our machine.

"What's he doing?" Betsy called.

"He's going to try to board," I replied.

"Should I stop for him?"

"No! Keep moving! Go as close as you can without hitting him."

"You know, steering this thing is not particularly *easy*, Mr. Derringer!" The irritation she felt was plain in her voice, and I did not blame her at all for it.

"I have faith in you, Miss Vanderhart!" I called back.

I climbed up out of the hatch and knelt atop the machine,

between the two rows of plates, ready to reach out and give Mr. Hancock a hand, should it prove possible. I stretched one arm out over the plates.

He ignored my hand – which was just as well, as he was well out of my reach – and waited until the hind legs stamped past him; then he turned and leapt for the tail, grabbing at the plates and using them to haul himself up.

A moment later we were face to face atop the creature's back, myself forward of the hatch facing aft, and Mr. Hancock behind it and facing forward.

"What are you doing?" I asked him.

"I think one of us should ride up top here, with a rifle," he said. "To discourage them a little. That means you need a third person."

I had to admit that was not an unreasonable suggestion. "Who rides shotgun, then, and who shovels coal?"

He hesitated.

Before he could reply, Betsy called up, "*One* of you best get down here and start shoveling, if you want to keep us moving! Pressure's dropping fast!"

"I'll go," Mr. Hancock said. "We don't have time to argue." With that he tossed his bowler down the hatch, then followed it, sliding down the ladder with surprising speed.

I scanned the horizon while he found the shovel, opened the firebox door, and began heaving coal into the furnace. I gave him time to make a good start, then called down, "When you have a moment to spare, you might hand me up my rifle. It's there by the big shaft on the right."

He did not waste a word, but simply passed the weapon up to me, and called, "Full speed ahead, Miss Vanderhart!"

Thus equipped, I settled in position with my feet braced on the rim of the hatch, the rifle in my hands, facing back in the direction we had come, as Betsy brought the machine back up to full speed.

Now that I had a few seconds to consider our situation, there were aspects of it that greatly puzzled me. The pursuing machines were presumably built to the same specifications as our own and would therefore not have any weapons on board; how, then, did they intend to stop us?

Furthermore, how did they intend to *catch* us? Wouldn't all of them only be capable of the same speed as our own machine? Could the others be fast enough to overtake us? Had we somehow been unfortunate enough to capture an inferior device? It was true we had not initially moved as quickly as we might have, but Betsy was now doing her best to coax the machine to its maximum speed.

I looked back, studying the rocks, trees, and brush. I could see that we were leaving a trail of broken branches and big flat footsteps that might have been enough for our pursuers to find us even if we were not leaving a trail of white smoke – but we were leaving a trail of white smoke, so there would be no point in looking for terrain where our path would be less obvious, as we had the previous night.

Then a movement caught my eye, and I looked up from the underbrush and saw something gleaming in the distance. A plume of smoke rose from it, much like the smoke that our own machine produced.

Then I realized that this mysterious apparition was not as far away as I had thought. It was golden-brown, rising high above the trees and shrubs, and had a semblance of a face at the top...

The Brontosaurus. I had forgotten for a time, even though that Brontosaurus had been the first of the monsters that Betsy and I had seen, that not all the Saints' mechanical dinosaurs were Stegosaurus. That thing behind us was undoubtedly the bizarrely long neck and blocky head of the mechanical Brontosaurus. It reminded me a little of a giraffe, though the proportions were quite different – and it was taller than any giraffe I had ever heard of.

Smoke was billowing from the back of its neck; I supposed that since a brontosaurus did not have convenient spinal plates to disperse the fumes its engines produced, Elder Baldwin had simply used the neck as a flexible smokestack.

This creature was following us and seemed to be gaining slightly.

But why was it gaining? Why did it have any more speed than we did? And was it only the Brontosaurus, or were the Stegosaurs also gaining?

I ducked my head down into the hatch and called to Betsy, "Is there some reason the other dinosaurs might be faster than we are?"

"*I* don't know," she exclaimed. "There could be. Better lubrication, a better grade of coal, more experienced crew – any of those might make a difference. I don't claim to have mastered this thing, Tom, only to be able to keep it moving in the right direction. They might even have altered the gearing to favor speed over power; I think I can see how it could be done." She glanced upward at one of the spinning shafts, then back over her shoulder. "Or maybe they just changed the setting on the governors. I don't know how much of a safety margin is built into those things."

None of those, save the more experienced operators, had occurred to me, but then, I was not an engineer. "Could they have done *all* of those things?" I asked. "Improved the lubrication, loaded better fuel, and the rest?"

"Probably."

"And how much of an advantage would that give them?"

"I told you, I don't know!" Betsy snapped. "Quite possibly a large one, but I just don't know what these things are capable of."

"Thank you," I replied. I did not want her to feel unappreciated, since we could not have taken the creature at all without her knowledge and ability. Then I lifted myself back out of the hatch and stared back up the slopes.

The Brontosaurus was definitely gaining.

But then something else burst out of the trees, along the same path we had taken - a Stegosaurus. Its coppery scales glittered in the sun, and a dozen thin trails of smoke and steam were rising from its spinal plates. That, too, was gaining on us.

I knew there was no sense in yelling. I leaned back toward the hatch and called, "Betsy? Can we go any faster?" I tried very hard to keep my voice calm.

"Not unless we raise more steam," she said.

"And how do we do that?"

"Shovel more coal, of course!"

"There's not all that much left," Hancock broke in, sounding worried. "At the rate we're burning it, I don't think it will last all the way to Ogden. Water's low, too."

"Then I think we have a problem."

"Can we find somewhere to hide it?" Mr. Hancock asked. "If we do that we can leave the machine out of sight somewhere and come back for it with a wagonload of coal..."

"That is not going to work," I said.

"Why not? What's happening?" Betsy asked.

"The other dinosaurs are chasing us, as Mr. Hancock came to tell us, and as you may have guessed from my questions, they appear to be faster than we are. They are already in sight; there's no way we could hide the machine in time, not the way this thing is smoking, and the way it glitters in the sun."

Betsy and Mr. Hancock exchanged glances.

"What are they going to do if they catch up to us?" Betsy asked.

"I don't know, but I doubt it will be anything we like."

"I assume this confounded machine is bulletproof," Mr. Hancock said.

"I would think so, yes." That could well be why the Saints had not simply sent armed men on horseback; we would have been able to ignore them and march on as their bullets bounced harmlessly from the metal scales.

But that still didn't explain what they planned to do instead, or why they had sent the dinosaurs. Mr. Hancock gave voice to exactly what I was thinking. "Then what can they do?" he said. "We'll close the hatch and just keep going."

"So long as the coal and water hold out, anyway," Betsy said.

I could not think of anything reassuring to say in response to that, so I did not say anything.

Mr. Hancock, though, asked, "Is there a route we could take where they wouldn't be able to follow?"

"Aren't the other machines the same as this one?" Betsy asked.

I lifted my head and looked behind us. "Well, the one... no, the two Stegosaurus I can see appear to be virtually identical to our own. The Brontosaurus is quite a bit larger." I observed, but did not say, that they were all coming closer at a dismaying pace.

"There's a Brontosaurus?" Betsy asked.

"Oh, I know I mentioned that!" Mr. Hancock said.

"You did, there is, and it's gaining on us," I replied. "That's the one we saw from the stockade wall, Betsy."

"Oh, of course," she replied. "Well, maybe I can find a path where it won't fit." She added, "But I don't see what I can do about other Stegosauruses."

"Is that the correct plural?" I asked.

"How should *I* know?" Betsy snapped. "Honestly, Tom, sometimes you worry about the most ridiculous things!"

"I don't suppose it matters at the moment, but when I write this adventure up for the Pierce Archives I'd prefer to have my terminology correct."

"You're assuming we'll get out of this alive," Mr. Hancock said, sounding a little peevish.

"Why, yes, Mr. Hancock, I am. These men pursuing us are not monsters; I would think they would prefer not to commit murder."

"It's not murder if it's self-defense," Mr. Hancock retorted.

"We're stealin' their confounded machine, and a man's got a right to defend his property."

I grimaced. "May I remind you, Mr. Hancock, that this theft was entirely *your* idea."

"I admit it." He clanged the coal shovel against a pipe, I believe inadvertently. "Now that I think about it, it may not have been the best idea I've ever had. I'd do the same thing if I had it to do over, though. I think the federal marshals deserve to know what these folks are up to, and after that hellish winter I wasn't inclined to go back empty handed. Besides, I really *did* think they might have stolen these contraptions somewhere, rather than built them. Honestly, who would have thought a bunch of settlers could build a thing like this? It's not as if they had Thomas Edison working with them!"

I had nothing useful to say in response to that, so I took another look behind us. The other dinosaurs were closing on us – not at any tremendous rate, but noticeably and steadily. I tried to estimate how long it would be before they would catch up.

"I'd say we have about half an hour before they reach us," I called down into the bowels of the machine. "An hour at the most. If anyone has a brilliant idea of how we might escape them, I would say this is a good time to put it into effect."

"What did you say about adjusting the machinery, Miss Vanderhart?" Mr. Hancock asked.

"I said that better lubrication might help," she replied. "Do you see an oil can back there?"

"No," Mr. Hancock said with a grimace. "Can't say for sure I'd know one if I saw it."

"Well, I don't know if it would be safe to use it while the engines are running, in any case," Betsy said. "Are there any adjusting knobs on the governors?"

"Any what on the what?"

"Adjusting knobs. Like the knob on a lamp, Mr. Hancock, the one to raise or lower the wick. And the governors are those spinning devices; they regulate the pressure in the various systems."

"I don't see any knobs."

"There might be fittings one works with a wrench, rather than a simple knob," I suggested.

"There might be, at that," Betsy agreed.

"And what would *those* look like?" Hancock asked.

"Oh, blast," I said. I turned and half-climbed, half-slid down the ladder into the gloomy, smoky interior of the machine, then looked at the governors, squeezing in beside Hancock and peering over his shoulder.

I saw five governors in all – a large one atop the main boiler that I had noticed right from the first, another much smaller one on either side, and then two down at ankle level on clusters of pipes leading toward the creature's front legs. None had any obvious means of adjustment. All were spinning at fairly high speeds.

"I don't see anything promising," I called to Betsy.

"Then I don't know how we might go any faster."

"Well, keep us moving," I said. Then I remounted the ladder.

Once back atop the machine, I took another look at our pursuers. They were definitely going to reach us in closer to a half-hour than an hour, I thought.

I realized that I did not see anyone atop the Stegosauruses, as I was atop ours; in fact, I did not see any humans at all beyond our own threesome. It was like some prehistoric scene, before humanity first arrived in North America, with these great behemoths charging across an uninhabited landscape. Was there some *reason* their operators remained hidden? Did they know something I did not?

I hoped not, and as I had no desire to return to the cramped and malodorous interior I remained where I was, hoping that something might happen to save us from capture or worse.

Chapter Seventeen

The Clash of Monsters

When the nearest of the other Stegosauruses came within fifty yards or so, behind and to our right, I took a deep breath and shouted as loudly as I could, "Might we talk this over?"

No one replied; I saw no sign that anyone had heard me over the thumping of huge metal feet and the monstrous din of the machinery inside each contraption.

We were marching our own vehicle up a slope at that point, approaching a pass in the range ahead. While I was unsure of our exact location, my best estimate was that crossing the pass would bring us in sight, or nearly so, of the village of Huntsville, the only town that I knew lay between ourselves and Ogden – though another mountain range separated the two communities. If we could get through the pass I had some hope that our pursuers would fall back, in the interest of maintaining as much secrecy as they could for their enterprise.

I wondered where Mr. Cartwright had gotten to; there was no sign of him or our three remaining mules. Mr. Hancock had said he was hiding, but I wondered where.

Wherever he was, it did not appear he would be able to

provide any assistance; we were on our own.

I ducked my head back through the hatch. "Betsy," I said, "you suggested that adjusting the governors would allow us greater speed. How would that work?"

"Tom, is this *really* the best time for an engineering lesson?"

"It may be."

She sighed. "The governors help regulate the pressure in the boiler and the lines that supply steam to the legs. In a locomotive or stationary engine you would generally have only a single governor, but in *this* thing the other four help keep the system balanced."

"*How* do they regulate the pressure?"

"Oh, it's simple. Ingenious, really, a classic bit of good engineering that's been used on practically all steam engines for the last century or so. The governor is the cap on a line from the boiler, and as pressure rises, steam is forced out through a small valve that turns the governor and makes it spin. There are two weights on arms, and the faster the governor spins, the more the spinning lifts those weights. When there's no pressure they hang down vertically on either side, not moving, but when it spins they stand out, until at maximum pressure the arms are completely horizontal."

"Yes, and then?" I said, encouragingly.

"Well, those arms are connected to relief valves. The higher they rise, the wider the valves open to relieve the pressure. As pressure drops there's less to make them spin, so they drop back down a little, and the relief valves partially close again. It's a brilliant bit of design that makes the engine self regulating. A governor prevents the pressure from getting high enough to be dangerous. If we could adjust them so that it requires more pressure to lift the arms and open those pressure relief valves, we would have more power to drive the dinosaur's legs, and we could walk faster."

"But you said higher pressure could be dangerous?"

"Well, of course! If it gets *too* high the boiler will explode. But unless Elder Baldwin was suicidal or otherwise insane, there's a margin of safety, and we could adjust it some. I assume that's what the other dinosaurs did. Of course, we don't know how *much* we could adjust it. The gauges should give us some idea, though."

"Explode?" Mr. Hancock interjected. He gave the boiler a worried glance. "It could explode?"

"Of course," Betsy answered. "*Any* steam engine will explode if you build up enough pressure and don't provide a relief valve." Just then the entire machine swayed violently, and I gripped the sides of the hatch. Mr. Hancock let out a wordless yelp of dismay. "My apologies, gentlemen," Betsy called. "We stepped on a boulder. The terrain is a little rougher here." A moment later we returned to a more level stance and more even motion, and the steady thump of our monster's tread resumed.

"I thought we'd had it," Mr. Hancock muttered; I don't think Betsy heard him. I decided not to discuss his concerns and instead lifted my head up above the back-plates once again, to study our situation.

It was worse than I had realized. I found myself looking down at the head of another mechanical Stegosaurus, alongside us on our right, not ten feet away from where I sat. I turned to the other side and found another metallic head was even with the midpoint of our creature's tail. Even as I watched, it gained several inches. And a glance behind showed the final Stegosaurus only a little further back, coming up on our right side, while the gigantic Brontosaurus was perhaps thirty yards behind on the left.

I still did not quite see how they intended to *stop* us, though. We might be trapped between them, but that would not prevent us from moving forward.

A lingering hope that we might yet talk matters out peacefully prompted me to shout, "Hey, there! Open up!"

As before, there was no response.

I decided the time had come to employ more drastic tactics.

I lifted my rifle to my shoulder and took aim at our left-hand companion's gleaming bronze neck, careful to avoid any risk of striking its crew or its boiler should my shot somehow penetrate its armor.

I fired, and as I had expected the bullet ricocheted harmlessly from the metal scales, whining away into the surrounding mountains.

None of our foes gave any sign they were aware of my action. The machine I had shot at was now up to our own creature's hips. On the right, the other Stegosaurus was up to our beast's shoulders. I watched as they stomped heavily along on either side.

And then the one on the left, now even with our own conveyance, swerved to the right, slamming into our flank with a tremendous clangor. Our machine shuddered and swayed.

"What was *that*?" Betsy shouted.

"They sideswiped us!" I called back. "They've caught up to us, one on each..."

I did not finish my sentence because the Stegosaurus to our right had now swerved, as well, and the bone-rattling collision cut off my final word.

And then the one on the left struck again, and we were pinned between the two, the three machines marching in lockstep, side by side.

"I'm losing control, Tom! I tried to turn aside, and I can't!"

"They have us trapped between them," I replied, grabbing at the armor plates on either side to steady myself as the three monsters trembled against one another, swaying unsteadily. "Just keep moving forward!"

"I don't know..." She did not finish whatever she had been going to say, as the other two machines, first the one on the left and then the one on the right, ground to a halt. Our own beast struggled to continue, forelegs scraping against the metal flanks pinning it on either side, but was unable to advance against the dead weight of the others.

"Damn!" I said. "They've pinned us." Any chance of abandoning our machine and making a run for it was gone; they would be able to catch us easily. I leaned down and called to Betsy, "Do you have any ideas of what we might do?"

"I don't even know what's going on!" she said. "I can't see anything in the glass."

"There's another machine on each side," I explained. "They've stopped, with their legs in front of ours, and are holding us back."

"Could we do something to increase power and push all three forward?" Mr. Hancock asked.

"I don't know!" Betsy exclaimed, clearly frustrated. "I don't know enough about these engines!"

"Here," Mr. Hancock said, reaching for one of the spinning governors. "What if I were to hold...ow!"

He had tried to grab the spinning arms, but had snatched his hand back.

"What happened?" I asked.

"It's hot! And it must be heavier than I thought – that *hurt* when it hit me!"

"Well, of course it did!" Betsy called back. "Those things are regulating the engines that drive this whole monstrous pile of machinery. That's a huge amount of power."

"What if we *did* stop them from spinning and shut them down?" I asked. "Would that give us more power?"

"Well, yes, right up until the boiler exploded!" Betsy retorted.

"Well, *that's* no..." I began. But then I stopped in mid-sentence. I considered for a moment. We were trapped, and even if we were to somehow escape that trap, we did not have enough coal to get the Stegosaurus to Ogden. I could not see any way to get the machine there – but I had an idea of how we might perhaps get there. I called down, "Mr. Hancock! Stealing this machine was your idea, but it does not appear we will be able to get it to Ogden. Given that, would you rather see it returned to its owners, or destroyed?"

"I...Derringer, are you mad?"

"No, sir, I am considering our options. If we surrender this machine, I am not at all sure what our pursuers will do with us. I doubt very much that we will be able to elude them long enough to reach Ogden, and we might wind up as prisoners, or they might simply shoot us. If we were to blow it up, though, I think we might well escape in the resulting confusion."

"If we aren't killed in the explosion!" Betsy cried.

"That *is* the tricky part," I admitted. I was about to say more when I heard a loud clang. I turned to see that the hatch between the spinal plates of the Stegosaurus on our right had been thrown open.

"Ahoy!" an unfamiliar voice called. I could not see who spoke; he kept his head below the protective plates, presumably to avoid gunfire.

"Ahoy, yourself," I shouted back.

"Surrender yourselves, and you won't be harmed! We only want our machine back."

"You'll let all five of us go on to Ogden unhindered?"

"Five?" Mr. Hancock said.

"Shh!" Betsy told him.

"It would be terrifically crowded with *five* people in here!"

"It would only be four; Tom's up on top."

"Still..."

I ignored their discussion and listened for a response from our pursuer.

The Saints' representative hesitated before replying, "I fear we cannot do that. We can't allow you to warn the marshals about our machines, or inform them where our refuge is. But we mean you no harm. You will be held, but you will be treated well."

I had already heard Betsy's opinion of another imprisonment, and I was not much more enthusiastic about the prospect than she was. "Let me confer with my companions," I said. Then I ducked down into the hot, malodorous interior.

Before either Betsy or Mr. Hancock could speak, I asked, "If we tie down the governors, how long will it be before the boilers explode?"

Betsy blinked at me, her mouth open; I had never before seen her at such a loss. Then she gathered her wits, closed her mouth, and turned to study the gauges.

"I can't give you an exact number," she said. "I don't know how much strain they can take. We already have the pressure near the top of the safe operating range, though, and if Mr. Hancock shovels in the last of the coal and sets the dampers for maximum heat, I'd say it will take somewhere between ten minutes and half an hour."

"That's a wider range than I had hoped for," I said, "but it's a range I can work with. If it would take hours we wouldn't have a chance, and less than five minutes wouldn't give us time to get clear."

"It's the best I can do. I haven't had a chance to study this thing in detail."

"I know," I said. "But it's the only way I see to not wind up as captives. Give me a moment. And Mr. Hancock, see if you can stop the upper left-side governor with that heavy wrench."

Then I climbed back up and thrust my head out of the hatch again.

"Ahoy!" I called.

"Are you ready to surrender?" came the response.

"Well, not exactly," I said. "Three of us want to abandon ship, as it were, but our engineer and our boss are determined to stay. If you promise us a safe conduct, though, the rest of us will give up."

There was no immediate response, but I thought I could hear muffled voices – apparently my offer had provoked some discussion aboard the right-hand machine.

During these various conversations, I saw that the

brontosaurus had drawn up behind us and had come to a halt, its absurdly long neck stretching up above our tail, and its head almost directly above me, so that even if we had thrown our machinery into reverse we would have had no escape. (I confess I do not know whether it would have been *possible* to throw it into reverse while trapped between the two Stegosauruses; I had never had a chance to ask Betsy.) I also saw that the fourth and final Stegosaurus had circled around and was now positioned in front of our own, broad side on, so that if we had somehow broken free of the two on either side we would have collided with it and been unable to proceed. We were, in short, completely surrounded.

That actually suited my plans rather well.

The Stegosaurus on our right, the one with the open hatch, began thumping its spiked tail vigorously against the ground, and swinging its head back and forth. This was apparently a pre-arranged signal; a moment later the hatches on both the other Stegosauruses clanged open, heads peering cautiously out between the spinal plates. A third loud metallic clatter came from the Brontosaurus, and a head appeared between the monster's shoulder blades.

A rifle also appeared between the creature's shoulder blades, pointed at me. I set my own rifle on a crosspiece below the hatch and raised my hands.

"Wait there," the man in the right-hand machine called. Then he clambered up and hurried down his beast's tail, waving to the man in the Brontosaurus.

I waited patiently as he hurried from one creature to the next, explaining the situation. Below me, I could hear Betsy and Mr. Hancock shutting down the governors one by one, securing each one with leather straps from the machine's tool cabinet, whispering to one another while Betsy kept a careful eye on the gauges to be sure nothing would explode before we were ready.

I could hear her telling Mr. Hancock to leave the strap on the main governor loose until we were ready to go, allowing it to continue to spin, giving us a final safety margin. I hoped that she had estimated the strains correctly; I had no desire to be scalded to death by live steam if she had misjudged.

Finally the Saints' spokesman came back and stood alongside our own machine. "The three of you can go," he called. "Now, send your boss out to negotiate."

"Oh, I tried," I answered, "but he says...pardon me, sir, but he says he'll see you in Hell first."

He looked disconcerted, and before he could compose himself I climbed up out of the hatch, then stood atop the back of the mechanical Stegosaurus with my hands raised. I looked down into the interior. "Whoever comes next, could you pass me up my rifle?"

Mr. Hancock passed the weapon up barrel first, so that my hold would be as unthreatening as possible. I accepted it and carefully did not shift to a more natural hold, but stepped back toward the tail as he climbed up out of the machine.

Betsy left her place at the controls and made her way back to the ladder, but paused long enough to yank tight the leather strap on the final governor, bringing its spinning to an abrupt halt, locking down the two weighted arms and closing tight the relief valve. Then she, too, emerged, glancing nervously down at the already-straining machinery.

That glance added verisimilitude to my ruse. "Our boss is not too happy with us, sir," I called. "He's calling us traitors and waving his Colt about. We don't want to be around if he starts shooting. May we go?"

"Fine," the spokesman called, gesturing with his weapon. "Go ahead. But not too far."

That last comment made it clear they still intended to take us prisoner. I hoped the coming explosion would be enough to distract them from that.

I led the way as the three of us hurried down the monster's tail, then turned aside and passed behind the tail of the machine on our right. The spokesman barely glanced at us as he cupped his hands around his mouth and called, "You in there! Give yourselves up!"

"I don't think Mr. Beckwith is going to do that," I said loudly, as we marched briskly away.

When we had gone perhaps fifty yards beyond the surrounding creatures Betsy looked back over her shoulder, then murmured, "Are they really going to just let us walk away?"

In fact, no one seemed to be paying any attention to us at all; they were all focused solely on the machine we had just abandoned. "I doubt it. They probably think they can recapture us easily once they have all five dinosaurs under their control," I replied.

"They probably can," Mr. Hancock retorted.

"I think they may have more urgent problems in a few minutes." I began to pick up the pace. "Betsy, how much longer do you think that boiler will hold?"

"I don't..." she began, but before she could complete her sentence our just-abandoned machine exploded with an earth-shaking thud and a hissing roar of escaping steam that left my ears ringing. Scraps of metal showered the area around us – most of them, fortunately, no bigger than a few copper scales. I turned to look back.

The top half of our machine had burst open, revealing a tangled mass of broken pipes and twisted steel frames, and a cloud of flame and smoke was billowing from that opening, spiraling around a white pillar of steam. A flying chunk of debris had smashed into the head of the Brontosaurus, and that head now dangled at a ridiculous angle from the wavering column of the creature's neck, coal smoke streaming around it. The Stegosauruses in front and on either side appeared largely intact, but had all been knocked off their feet by the explosion, and now lay on their sides.

Teddy Hancock was stooping down for something, but I did

not see what it was.

"Can they right themselves?" I asked Betsy. My voice sounded muffled to me, as my ears had not recovered from the blast.

"I didn't see any mechanism for that," she answered, and it sounded as if her voice came from beneath a pillow.

"In that case," I said, "I think the time has come for us to run."

Chapter Eighteen

Our Return to Ogden

We suited our actions to my words and lit out to the southwest, up the side of a mountain. Even with my damaged ears I could hear angry shouting behind us, so I knew at least some of the Saints had come through the blast relatively unhurt. I hoped none of them were seriously injured; I wished them no harm. I wondered how long it would take them to realize that we had not, in fact, left two companions aboard our now-destroyed vehicle.

Mostly, though, I ran – not flat out, because Betsy's shorter legs could not match my top speed, but at the best pace she could maintain. We ran until Mr. Hancock collapsed, panting, on the ground.

We had crested the shoulder of a mountain and were out of sight of the remains of the steam-powered dinosaurs, but I was not so foolish as to think we were out of danger. Anyone who came after us would be able to spot us readily enough, as the countryside here was relatively open, with no trees, but only tall grass and scattered shrubs.

"While I understand the need to catch your breath, Mr. Hancock," I said, "I trust you will not take long to do so." My hearing was returning to normal, and my voice was familiar once more.

"I'll be fine in a moment, Derringer," he said. He held up his hand, and I saw he was clutching a fragment of the demolished Stegosaurus - a strip of metal spangled with a dozen gleaming coppery scales that glittered in the sunlight. He glanced back the way we had come. "Do you think they'll chase after us?"

"I'd say it's fairly likely."

"Fine." He clambered back to his feet, then began lurching forward again.

We took a winding path, crossing bare outcroppings of stone when we could, to make tracking us more difficult, and I took the first opportunity to put a stand of maples behind us so that we would be less visible from the mountains we had crossed.

We pressed on until the sun was below the horizon, and the vivid colors of a spectacular sunset had largely faded away, then took shelter beneath a spreading box elder. We had no supplies with us beyond the contents of my pockets; most of what we had brought was in the packs aboard the mules. I had managed to retain my rifle, but little else. Even my almost-new hat was missing; I suspect it had been blown off by the concussion of the explosion, and I had not noticed at the time. I gave Betsy my coat, to serve as a blanket; I was glad that I had kept it on despite the heat from the Stegosaurus' furnace. We had no food, and the land did not provide any that we recognized as such, so we went to sleep hungry, but we had found a mountain stream that had slaked our thirst. If we had still been aboard our saurian conveyance, this would have been a good spot to refill the water tanks; as it was, only Mr. Hancock still had his canteen, but we did refill that.

As we retired, we wondered to one another what might have become of Mr. Cartwright and our three remaining mules; we had seen no sign of them since Teddy Hancock came galloping after us.

We also wondered whether the Saints would come to Ogden looking for us; they would almost certainly guess that that was our destination. The possibility of going somewhere else was broached, but we did not know where else we might go.

The next day we awoke before dawn, when the eastern sky was still gray, and set out again. Water remained relatively easy to find, but we were not able to find food, especially since we were reluctant to shoot at anything for fear our pursuers, if they existed, might hear.

We stumbled on as quickly as we could, with only the briefest rests. We did not speak much, as we were saving our breath for walking, but Betsy did remark at one point that it had been a shame to destroy such a magnificent machine, and Mr. Hancock replied that indeed it was, as it meant we had nothing to show for our adventures except the little souvenir he had grabbed. He displayed his prize to Betsy, who was not interested.

I ignored Teddy's comment and reminded Betsy that the Saints could probably salvage and restore the other dinosaurs, so the secrets of their engineering would not be lost.

On the third day I was beginning to be seriously concerned about our lack of sustenance, but that morning we spotted a settler's cabin, where we were made welcome by a rather puzzled young couple. They did not seem to find our tale of having been stranded when our horses ran off with our supplies to be very convincing, especially since we failed to devise a consistent and believable explanation of why we were out in the wilderness in the first place.

We were, we learned, on the outskirts of a town called Eden, which Mr. Cartwright had mentioned to us early in our expedition; it lay some short distance northwest of Huntsville, and Ogden was just beyond the next ridge, perhaps no more than fifteen miles away. We had wandered slightly off our intended course, but not dangerously so.

Our hosts refused payment, even though we must have seriously depleted their household supplies, so when we moved on I simply left two dollars on the table, under a napkin so that they would not find it in time to return it. I was glad I had kept my money in my pockets, and not tucked it away in the supplies we had left with the mules.

After our meal we gathered ourselves up and pressed on –
fifteen miles did not seem like too much to manage in the
remaining daylight hours, and we were eager to return to
civilization and to be done with those tiresome mountains. We
had not fully considered the terrain's effects on our pace, though,
and the last light of dusk was fading when we finally stumbled into
town and made our way through the dark and muddy streets to the
Reed Hotel.

The desk clerk made no comment about our disreputable
appearance, but merely attended to the business of assigning us
two adjacent rooms – one for Betsy, and one that Teddy Hancock
and I would share. I did not intend to let Mr. Hancock out of my
sight any longer than absolutely necessary until I had collected the
sum the committee had agreed to pay me for his safe return.

When the register had been signed, the clerk paused before
handing over the keys. "Oh, Derringer!" he said, upon seeing my
name. "I believe we have a message for you." He turned, still
holding the keys, and found a slip of paper in one of the
pigeonholes.

I held my breath in anticipation – was there a telegram from
my mother that had not reached us before our departure? But
no, the paper was not Western Union's familiar form, but a brief
scribbled note on plain paper. The clerk read it, then handed it
over.

"A Mr. Cartwright checked in late last night," he said. "He
asked us to let you know, should you come in, that he is in Room
Eleven and hopes to hear from you."

"Pete's here?" Mr. Hancock exclaimed. "How'd he get back
before us?"

"He had the mules," I pointed out. "And he probably took a
more direct route."

"Tom," Betsy said, "while I'm very glad to know that Mr.
Cartwright made it back safely, and I am well aware that we have

business to conclude, could we please just go to our rooms, wash up, and get some rest?"

"And supper," Mr. Hancock added.

I nodded, as my own preferences matched theirs. "If you see Mr. Cartwright," I told the clerk, "please inform him that I very much hope to see him tomorrow at breakfast. And could you have food sent to our rooms? Anything filling."

"Beer with it would be fine," Mr. Hancock interjected.

"We don't serve liquor," the clerk said.

"Mormons," Betsy reminded Mr. Hancock.

Mr. Hancock made a noise of disgust. "Well, whatever you have, then."

And that was that. We bathed, then dined in our rooms, and then went early to bed.

In the morning, when we had dressed – still in the same clothes, since we had no others – we went down to breakfast and were delighted to see Mr. Cartwright already there. Upon seeing us he rose with an exclamation of delight, and in seconds he and Mr. Hancock were embracing, clapping one another on the back and exchanging compliments.

All four of us took seats at the same table, and we began trading tales of our adventures with Mr. Cartwright. His story was much simpler than ours; the mechanical monsters had bypassed him in pursuit of their stolen companion, and he had then proceeded to Ogden unhindered. The three remaining mules were stabled behind the hotel, he assured me, and most of our supplies were intact and stored in Room Eleven.

My hat was gone, though; the faint hope that I had left it with the mules was frustrated. I had been fairly sure I had been wearing it aboard the Stegosaurus, but I had hoped my memory was playing tricks on me.

Betsy almost shrieked with delight at the knowledge that she had fresh clothing available; I could see her warring with herself as to whether she should continue to breakfast with us, or demand that Cartwright loan her his key so that she might hurry upstairs to change.

In the end hunger won out, perhaps assisted by the impropriety of making an unchaperoned visit to a man's hotel room.

The hotel's breakfast offerings were simple fare of indifferent quality, but at that point we really did not much care and set to voraciously once our food arrived. As a result, there was little conversation until we had all eaten our fill.

At last, though, Mr. Hancock leaned back in his chair and said, "It's good to be back in civilized territory!"

"And I, for one, am very glad to see you back here!" Mr. Cartwright said. "When I heard the explosion I feared the worst. An hour or two later I passed near enough that I could see that the machines had all been knocked higgledy-piggledy, and that at least one had been blown to bits, but I dared not go close enough to make out the details – there were at least half a dozen men hauling at the wreckage. I think they were trying to set one back on its feet."

"I think they'll need more than half a dozen men to do that," I said. "Those things must weigh several tons apiece."

"Well, they've got more than half a dozen men, back in that little fort of theirs," Hancock remarked. "If they aren't complete fools, they'll have sent someone to fetch more men, and horses, and perhaps some machinery to give them leverage." He sighed. "They'll probably have four of those things running in a few days."

"They won't be repairing *ours*, though," Betsy said, a trifle smugly.

"If that was yours in the center, no, they won't," Mr. Cartwright agreed. "It was scattered all over the hillside."

"I don't know whether they will be able to restore the head on the Brontosaurus, either," I said. "It looked pretty well smashed."

"It will run perfectly well without its head, though," Betsy pointed out.

Perhaps it was my lingering fatigue, but that struck me as irresistibly amusing, and I could not restrain a snort of laughter.

"Like a chicken with its head cut off," Mr. Hancock said, and at that *all* of us began laughing.

After a moment, though, we had sobered enough for the open laughter to give way to gentle smiles, and then even that vanished from Mr. Hancock's face.

"It's a shame, though, that I spent all those months out there in the wilderness, half freezing and half starving, and came back with nothing to show for it but this." He pulled his little keepsake out of his pocket and set it on the table. "I don't think any museums will be paying me for that!"

"You're alive," Betsy said.

"And you have a good tale to tell, as well as that souvenir," I said. "I suspect Mr. Pierce will pay a good sum for a written account for his archives."

"If you don't get to him with yours first."

"Oh, I won't do that," I said. "I *did* find what I went after, after all, and I expect the committee to make good on their promises, so I can afford to leave any other spoils to you."

"Oh? Including any fee for providing the marshals with the nature and location of that little fort the Mormons have built for themselves?"

There was a sudden silence. Betsy and I exchanged glances, while Mr. Cartwright sat bolt upright and stared at Mr. Hancock.

"Why would you do that?" he asked at last.

"Why would I do what?" Mr. Hancock asked, apparently genuinely puzzled.

"Why would you tell the federals about the refuge?"

"Well, I just said, didn't I? For the reward."

"You said before that you didn't care one way or the other about their refuge," I reminded him.

"You don't know whether there *is* a reward," Betsy said.

"They're not doing anyone any harm, Teddy," Mr. Cartwright

added.

"Well, I'd think *someone* in the governor's office would be willing to pay me for information on where to find a secret outpost of Danites!"

"They aren't Danites!" Mr. Cartwright exclaimed. "There *aren't* any Danites!"

"Well, they're the next best thing," Mr. Hancock insisted.

"They're just trying to protect their leader," I pointed out.

"A leader who kept eight women..." Betsy began.

"*Stop it!*" Mr. Cartwright burst out.

We all fell silent; then he turned to us one by one.

"Mr. Derringer," he said. "Do you intend to inform anyone of the existence of that refuge?"

I hesitated as I gathered my thoughts, then said, "Well, I think someone should tell Mr. Pierce, but he is the very soul of discretion, and unless he has some animus against your co-religionists of which I am utterly unaware, I doubt very much that he would trouble himself to inform the territorial authorities. Even if he were to do so, he might not be believed; many people assume that half of what we adventurers report is exaggeration or outright fiction." I grimaced. "Other than that, not only do I not see it as any of my business, but I am not at all certain I could find the place again, let alone describe its location well enough to guide anyone else to it. What's more, we did rob them of a very valuable machine, and to do them such a bad turn on top of that scarcely seems sporting."

He nodded, then turned to Betsy. "And you, Miss Vanderhart," he said. "Would you care to accompany me to Salt Lake City so that you might interview President Taylor's wives yourself? I think you'll find that none of them feel their husband has wronged or abused them."

"I don't..." She glanced at me, then back at Mr. Cartwright. "I don't think that will be necessary," she said. "Perhaps I have been hasty in judging the morals of others, when my own actions, as my mother has so vehemently told me, may not always have been above reproach. Further, it is, as Tom said, not really any of my business. Revealing the existence of their hiding place might well result in unnecessary bloodshed, and I would prefer not to have that on my conscience. But rest assured, Mr. Cartwright, if I learn that those men are taking hostile action against anyone, and not merely defending themselves, I will be happy to tell the authorities what I know." She glanced at me once more. "Though like Tom, I doubt I could find the place again. I am a mechanician, not an explorer."

Mr. Cartwright nodded and turned to Mr. Hancock. "Teddy," he said, "I am asking you as a friend, do not inform the federals."

"Damn it, Pete!" He glared at Mr. Cartwright. "I could probably get fifty dollars in gold for this story!"

"Is the money the *only* reason?"

"Well, I...I still don't think much of your people, Pete, yourself excluded, and I'm still half convinced that bunch out there are so close to being Danites that the difference doesn't amount to a tinker's dam, but if it weren't for the money..." He let his voice trail off and looked troubled; clearly, he did not really want to antagonize his friend.

"Teddy," Mr. Cartwright said, after a few seconds of awkward silence, "I think that the committee owes you some compensation for the risks you took on our behalf, and for the information you've brought back, even if we don't have anything to sell to Dr. Marsh or Mr. Cope or the museums back East. Suppose we paid you a hundred dollars, in gold if you like, to keep your findings confidential?"

"Oh, well..."

"Can he still sell the tale to Mr. Pierce?" I asked.

"I think that at the very least we can discuss it," Mr. Cartwright said.

"*Someone* should see that it gets into the Archive."

"I don't know whether a hundred dollars will cover it," Mr. Hancock said.

"It's more than you'd get from the federals, and you know it."

"Well..."

"I'll throw in any claim we might have to the mules," I said. "Betsy and I will be traveling by train and won't have any use for them."

"And I'll personally cover the hotel bill for all of you," Mr. Cartwright said.

That evoked a crooked grin. "Done," Mr. Hancock said. He and Mr. Cartwright reached across the breakfast table and shook hands, and the matter was settled.

I had one more concern. "Do you think those men will come to Ogden looking for us?" I asked Mr. Cartwright.

"I think that for the next few days they are going to be far too busy salvaging their machines to bother. Beyond that, though, I couldn't say. And I don't know whether they could find you here, in any case."

"At least one of them heard me called Mr. Derringer."

"That's unfortunate. Still, I don't think you need to worry immediately."

I nodded.

With that, we rose from our chairs and made our way upstairs to reclaim our belongings from Mr. Cartwright and to start the new day.

An hour later, both of us in relatively fresh clothing, Betsy and I headed for the Western Union office. Mr. Cartwright had assured us that he would be going there later in the day, to inform his fellow committee members of the situation and arrange for the payment of my fee, but he had other matters he wanted to attend to first. We had no other pressing concerns, so far as we knew, and we were eager to let our families know that we were both still alive.

Or at least, *I* was eager. Betsy remained uncertain of her

mother's attitude, which significantly dampened her enthusiasm.

As we made our way down the street I asked, "Are you sure you don't want to go to Salt Lake City with Mr. Cartwright to meet President Taylor's eight wives?"

Betsy shuddered slightly. "Quite sure," she said.

"It might be quite informative."

"Tom, I find it bad enough that most women choose to make themselves so thoroughly subordinate to their husbands, but to do so for a mere *eighth* of a husband is simply incomprehensible to me. And since I have no reason to doubt that Mr. Cartwright is correct in saying these women are indeed happy with their lot, I fear that if I were to speak to them I might well say something unforgivably rude. Or just start screaming."

I could not help but smile at that.

"I don't know that they are *happy* with their lot, at present," I said. "After all, Congress has declared their husband a criminal. But they are reported to be satisfied with their shared spouse. As for women who subordinate themselves to their husbands, is that not what the Bible instructs them to do?" I did not mean this seriously, as I trust she realized, but I could not resist a jab at her unorthodox beliefs, even though I shared many of them.

She started to reply, but all that came out was best rendered as "Mmmph," as she thought better of saying it aloud.

I did not want to tease her further, but I hoped that I had at least distracted her for a moment from her worries about her continuing estrangement from her mother.

We arrived at the telegraph office and waited our turn at the counter. I did not really expect anything to be waiting for us, but thought we should ask before composing our own messages, so when our turn came I stepped up and said, "Have you anything for Derringer or Vanderhart?"

"Vanderhart!" the clerk exclaimed. "Elspeth Vanderhart?"

Startled, I turned to Betsy, who nodded, too stunned to speak.

"Finally!" the clerk said. "I was afraid you might never turn up. And I think we have something for Derringer, too. J. Thomas Derringer, is it?"

"It is," I acknowledged.

"Wait here." He turned to one of the pigeonholes behind him, withdrew a stack of paper, and set it on the counter. "That's Vanderhart," he said. Then he returned to the pigeonholes.

Betsy did not wait before picking up her telegrams, though.

"It's from Mother," she said, studying the top one. "It's dated two weeks ago, the very day we left."

"What does it say? Is she continuing to berate you for daring to defend yourself?"

"No," Betsy said, and her voice broke in a way I had not heard since we left New York all those months ago. She did not offer any further explanation beyond handing me the first telegram.

"YOUR FATHER KIDNAPED," it said. "COME AT ONCE." The signature was MOTHER.

I stared at it, baffled. Professor Vanderhart, kidnapped? That made no sense.

The next in the stack, dated three days later, was slightly more explicit. DID YOU RECEIVE TELEGRAM QUESTION. YOUR FATHER HAS BEEN KIDNAPED STOP. PLEASE COME HOME AT ONCE STOP. BRING MR DERRINGER STOP.

Three days after that, OTHER SCIENTISTS ALSO MISSING STOP. COME AT ONCE STOP.

A day later, NO ONE ELSE TO ASK STOP. PLEASE COME HOME STOP.

There were seven from her mother in all, growing ever more frantic; the last had been sent just the day before.

And there was one from *my* mother in the stack, as well. DEAR MISS VANDERHART, YOUR FATHER REALLY HAS BEEN TAKEN STOP. YOUR MOTHER IS HEARTBROKEN STOP. THIS IS NOT A TRICK TO LURE YOU HOME STOP. THE PROFESSOR AND

OTHER SCIENTISTS ARE MISSING STOP.

I had just finished reading that when the clerk handed me three of my own - two from my mother, and one from Mrs. Vanderhart. I read Mrs. Vanderhart's first.

I KNOW BETSY ANGRY WITH ME STOP. PLEASE BRING HER HOME ANYWAY STOP. COME WITH HER STOP. WE NEED YOUR HELP STOP.

My mother's were longer and more detailed. She assured me that she and Mary Ann were fine, and that they hoped to hear from me soon, but understood that I probably wasn't near a telegraph office. Several scientists had gone missing over the past few months, including Professor Vanderhart, and several adventurers were taking an interest - and *they* were starting to disappear, as well. The professor had returned from his voyage to the South Seas more or less on schedule, but a fortnight later, without warning, he had simply vanished. He had gone to see a guest off at the railroad station, and had not been seen nor heard from since. Mrs. Vanderhart was hysterical and wanted me to investigate; she did not trust any of the others who were already pursuing the matter.

I thought it was rather odd that she apparently trusted me, since she had more or less accused me of luring her daughter into a life of debauchery and murder, but I do not pretend to understand how her mind worked.

"It seems we will be heading East immediately," I said.

Betsy nodded, but then paused. "What about your pay?" she asked.

"They can wire it to me." I set the telegrams down on the counter and said, "I'll reply to these two." I pointed to my mother's missives.

"Very good," the clerk said, readying his pencil and a form.

"'Dear Mother'," I said. "'On our way.' That's it, just those three words."

"Right," he said. "And you, Miss?"

"The same thing," she said. "To *my* mother." She tossed her stack of messages on the counter.

The clerk nodded, calculated our bill, and collected our payment. We left.

Betsy started directly toward the rail station, but I caught her arm. "We have a few things to do first," I said. "Collect our luggage from the hotel, settle a few matters with Messrs. Hancock and Cartwright, and so on. And there's the small matter that I don't have enough cash left to pay for our tickets."

"Oh," Betsy said. "Oh, of course."

Fortunately, our erstwhile companions understood the need for haste, and Mr. Cartwright was able to forward me a portion of what he and his fellows owed me, promising that the balance would be wired directly to Tobias Arbuthnot, for deposit to my bank account.

These matters took longer than I had hoped, certainly longer than Betsy wanted them to, so it was not until the following morning that we found ourselves on the platform, waiting to board the Union Pacific express.

And in our rush, I had not found time to buy a new hat. I headed East bare-headed – but at least we were headed East.

– THE END –

About the Author:

Lawrence Watt-Evans has been a full-time writer for more than forty years, with about fifty novels and well over a hundred short stories to his credit, as well as assorted essays, poems, comic books, and so on. His story "Why I Left Harry's All-Night Hamburgers" won the 1988 Hugo for short story, as well as the Asimov's Readers Award. He lives in Bainbridge Island, Washington with his wife.

His website is at www.watt-evans.com.

www.ingramcontent.com/pod-product-compliance
Lightning Source LLC
Chambersburg PA
CBHW061323200626

46813CB00017B/2833